jim thompson
the criminal

James Meyers Thompson was born in Anadarko,
Oklahoma, in 1906. He began writing fiction at a very
young age, selling his first story to *True Detective*
when he was only fourteen. In all, Jim Thompson
wrote twenty-nine novels and two screenplays (for
the Stanley Kubrick films *The Killing* and *Paths
of Glory*). Films based on his novels include: *Coup
de Torchon (Pop. 1280)*, *Serie Noire (A Hell of a
Woman)*, *The Getaway*, *The Killer Inside Me*, *The
Grifters*, and *After Dark, My Sweet*. A biography
of Jim Thompson will be published by Knopf.

the
criminal

jim thompson

VINTAGE CRIME / **BLACK LIZARD**

vintage books • a division of random house, inc. • new york

First Vintage Crime/Black Lizard Edition, January 1993

Library of Congress Cataloging-in-Publication Data
Thompson, Jim, 1906–1977.
The criminal/by Jim Thompson. — 1st Vintage Crime/Black Lizard ed.
p.   cm. — (Vintage Crime/Black Lizard)
ISBN 0-679-73314-0
I. Title.   II. Series.
PS3539.H6733C75   1993
813'.54 — dc20   92-56369   CIP

Manufactured in the United States of America
10   9   8   7   6   5   4   3   2   1

There is thy gold, worse poison to men's souls,

Doing more murders in this loathsome world,

Than these poor compounds that thou mayst not sell.

I sell thee poison, thou hast sold me none.

Romeo and Juliet, Act V, Sc. 1

the
criminal

allen talbert 1

It had been a pretty good day in many ways, so I might have known it would turn out bad. If you've read any papers lately I guess you know that it did. It's always that way with me, it seems like. I've never known it to fail. I'll wake up feeling rested and be able to eat breakfast for a change, and maybe I'll even get a seat on the 8:05 into the city. And it'll go on like that all day—no trouble, everything rocking along fine. My kidneys won't bother me. I won't get those crazy headaches up over my eyes. Then, I'll come home, and somehow or another, between the time I get there and the time I go to bed, something will happen to spoil it all. Always. Anyway, it seems like always. There'll be a dun from the Kenton Hills Sewer District or a gopher will have eaten up what blamed little lawn we have left or Martha will break her glasses. Or something.

Take the night before last, for example. I'd had a pretty good day that day—as good as any day can be, now. Then, after dinner, I sit down to read the paper, and—bingo!—I hop right back up again. Martha's glasses were in the chair, or, rather, what was left of 'em. Both lenses were broken.

"Oh, my goodness," she said, fluttering around and picking up the pieces. "Now, how in the world did that happen?"

"How did it happen?" I said. "How did it *happen?* You leave your glasses in my chair, and then you wonder how it happens when they get broken."

"I must have left them on the arm of the chair," she said. "You must have brushed them into the seat when you sat down. Oh, well, I needed some new ones anyway."

I looked at her, taking it all so calm and casual, and

3

something seemed to snap inside my head. I wanted to hurt her, to hurt someone and she was the nearest thing at hand.

"So you needed some new ones," I said. "That's all you've got to say. You throw fifteen dollars down the drain, and it doesn't make any difference to you, does it? You'll never change, will you? If you weren't so scatter-brained, if you'd kept an eye on Bob instead of letting him run wild and do as he pleased he wouldn't have—"

Her face went white, then red. "And what about you? What kind of a father are you to—to—" Her hand went up to her mouth, pushing back the words. "D-Don't," she whispered. "I—I d-don't need any glasses. I can't read any more, anyway. I can't—all I can think about is . . . Oh, Al! Al!"

I put my arms around her, and she tried to pull away— but not very hard—and then she buried her face against my shirtfront, and she cried and cried. I didn't try to stop her. I wished I could have cried myself. I stood holding her, patting her on the head now and then; noticing how gray she had gotten. It was funny, strange I mean. You hear about someone turning gray almost overnight, and you think, oh, that's a lot of nonsense. It couldn't really happen, not to normal people anyway. And then it does happen, right to your own wife, and I don't imagine they come more normal than Martha.

It's like it is with Bob. With Bob's trouble. You hear about some fifteen-year-old boy killing a neighbor's girl—raping and strangling her, and you think, well, I'm pretty well off after all. My boy may be a little wild but . . . *but Bob was never really wild; he was just all boy, I guess, just about average* . . . but my boy would never do a thing like that. That could never happen in our family. He—

Your wife couldn't turn gray overnight, and your fifteen-year-old couldn't do what that other fifteen-year-old did. The idea is so crazy that—well, you just laugh when you think about it. And then. . .

"Al," Martha whispered. "Let's move away from here!"

"You bet," I said. "We'll go to work on it tomorrow. We'll

move way off somewhere, clear to the other side of the country."

I was just talking, of course, and she knew it. I couldn't start in all over at my age, get a job that would support us. We don't have any money to move on. I had to borrow against the house to pay that lawyer. All the equity we've got in it now you could stuff in your ear.

Anyway, moving wouldn't do much good. Because it isn't the other people so much, the way they talk and act and the way we imagine they talk and act: it's not them so much as it is ourselves. Wondering about it, and not being sure. Sure like you've got to be about a thing like that.

"Al," Martha whispered, "h-he—he didn't do it, did he?"

"Of course, he didn't," I said. "It's too ridiculous to think about."

"I know he didn't do it, Al!"

"I do, too. We both know it."

"Why, he just couldn't! I mean, why—why—how could he, Al?"

"I don't know," I said. "I—it doesn't matter. He didn't, so there's no sense wondering about it. We've got to stop it, Martha. We've got to stop wondering and talking and—and—"

"Of course, dear," she said. "We won't say another word. We both know he didn't, that he couldn't have. Why, my goodness, Al! How could our Bob . . . ?"

"SHUT UP!" I said. "Stop it!"

It ended as it usually ends. We kept telling each other that he hadn't done it, and it was crazy even to think he had. Finally, we went to bed, and all night long, whenever I woke up, I heard her mumbling and tossing. And in the morning I caught her looking at me worriedly, and she asked me if I'd slept well. So I guess I must have been doing some mumbling and tossing myself.

Well . . .

I guess there's no right place to begin this. A thing like this, it probably starts a long way back, before you were ever married probably and ever had a son named Bob. And maybe you didn't have too much to do with it yourself; you didn't have too much control over it. You just rock along, doing the things you have to, and you get kind of startled sometimes when you stand off and look at yourself. You think, my God, that isn't me. How did I ever get like that? But you go right ahead, startled or not, hating it or not, because you don't actually have much to say about it. You're not moving so much as you are being moved.

Maybe I'm making excuses, but what I'm trying to say is that it might have begun with another person. Or other people. My parents, say. Or their parents. Or people I'd never met in my life. It . . . I don't know. I couldn't say. There's no way of telling, and one beginning place is probably as good as another. So maybe I'd better lead off with the start I had.

Maybe I'd better go back to *the* day it happened. The day that had been a pretty good one until it did happen. If I start right in with the beginning of the day and follow it on through, maybe . . . maybe I'll spot something.

I do that down at the office sometimes, down at the Henley Terrazzo & Tile Company. I mean, the books will be off a few cents when I try to strike a balance, so I'll take a new set of transcript sheets and recopy my figures, checking them off item by item. And sooner or later I'll find the error. It'll pop up at me. Providing, of course, that it's in that day's work.

Well, I've told you I'd had a good night's sleep and a pretty good breakfast. Bob and I ate together *that* day, and I kind of joked with him a little, like I don't often have the time nor the inclination for, and afterwards he walked part of the way to the station with me on his way to school.

It had been a long time since he'd done that. In fact, I couldn't remember when the last time was he'd done it, It used to be, back when he was in the grades, we'd walk together almost every morning, It put him to school earlier than he had to be, but he insisted on doing it, He'd actually get upset if Martha let him sleep and I'd go off without him.

Well, though, as I say, that had been a couple years ago, Or even longer I guess. Back in those days, up until the time, say, he was about in the sixth grade, he not only walked with me in the morning but he'd be at the train to meet me in the evening. It seemed he'd rather be with me than he would kids his own age. Quite a few people commented on it. I remember Martha's mother was visiting us one spring, and she couldn't get over it. She said she'd never seen anyone that was such a Daddy's boy.

A very fine woman, Martha's mother. She passed on— let's see—sixteen months ago, next June. No, fifteen months ago. The way I remember the date is that I had the undertaker spread his bill through twelve equal installments, and . . . But we don't need to go into that. She was a very fine old lady, and I was glad to do what I could.

Well, as I was saying, that was the way Bob had *used* to be. Back during the war when there was more terrazzo and tile work than you could shake a stick at, and your only problem was priorities. I'll tell you: things were a lot different in those days. I didn't draw any more salary than I do now, but the bonuses almost doubled it. I didn't work half so hard and I made almost twice as much as I do these days. If I wanted to take an afternoon off, I took it. Not very often, but Henley never let out a peep when I did.

One time I took a whole day off, a Friday. I had Martha and Bob meet me in town Thursday night, and we stayed the whole weekend—Friday, Saturday and Sunday. Three days and four nights. I got us a couple of connecting rooms at a pretty good hotel, but we weren't in 'em much except to sleep. At least, Bob and I weren't. Martha would say, "You men, I just can't keep up with you." So we'd leave her at the hotel to catch up on her rest, and we'd go out on the town by ourselves.

Saturday morning we went out by ourselves; we went out for breakfast together. I bet Bob that I could eat more hotcakes than he could, and we had three stacks apiece—a tie—before we called it quits. Nine hotcakes apiece, mind you, not to mention the butter and syrup. If I did that now, it would kill me.

After breakfast, we went to a penny arcade and I bought five dollars worth of change. It was noon before we'd spent it all, so we had a big feed at an Italian restaurant, and then we strolled around and finally wound up in a shooting gallery. I kind of went hog wild in there. Bob and I were shooting a contest with each other, and the first thing I knew I'd spent twenty dollars. It was quite a bit of money even for good times, and Bob was a little scared when I told him about it. "Gosh," he said, sort of shakily, "I'll bet Mom will be mad."

"I'll bet she won't," I said. "Not unless she's a mind reader."

He looked up at me, a trifle puzzled. And I nodded and gave him the wink. Then I grinned, and after a minute he grinned. And that was the end of the matter. I didn't need to tell him to keep quiet about the money. He caught on right away. I maybe shouldn't say it, but they didn't make kids sharper than Bob.

Well, we had a fine time that weekend. Monday morning I took Bob and Martha to the station, and we had breakfast there before they caught their train. Martha asked me if I wasn't afraid I'd be late for work.

"So I'll be late," I said. "What of it?"

"But won't Mr. Henley say something?"

"I hope he does," I said. "He gives me a little trouble, and I'll tell him where to head in."

Bob's eyes got as big as saucers. He looked at me like I was John L. Sullivan, or someone like that.

I can't put my finger on the exact time when he began to change, but it was some time after the war. It wasn't much of a change at first—he'd just kind of avoid me, and not have much to say when I was around. And when I said something to him, he acted like I was picking on him. I couldn't say the smallest word to him about why he wasn't doing better in school, for Pete's sake, or why he couldn't comb his hair without being told sixteen times, without him getting sullen. Anything I said, it was that way.

He went on like that, getting a little more stubborn and mulish, it seemed, for every inch he grew, and then one day a couple years ago, just about the time he was thirteen and starting into high school, well . . . he changed completely. He really didn't seem like Bob after that.

On that day that Bob seemed to change, I'd had a pretty rough time of it. You probably think there's been plenty of building since the war ended, and there has been. But it's mostly residential stuff, and the money just isn't to be made in that kind of work. Oh, you make money, sure, but it's nothing like it was during the war. Even the commercial stuff you get now is a darned far cry from the government-contract jobs. You go to a man now and say, Sure, I'll do such and such a job for you. Cost plus ten per cent. You say that to him, and then you'd better start running because he's liable to throw something at you.

Well, so business hadn't been anything like it was during the war—and it still isn't, believe me, not in tile and terrazzo anyway—and getting along with Henley was like trying to get along with a bear with a toothache. He was after me every day about something. If he wasn't riding me, he was watching me, looking for something to hop on me about. I'm not exaggerating. It was like that, and it still is.

I'd prepare the bid on a job, and possibly we'd be low by as little as four cents a square foot. Just barely low enough to get the job. But that wouldn't be good enough for Henley, I'd lost the company three and nine-tenth cents per, to hear him tell it; if I'd been on the beam I'd have made our bid only a tenth of a cent low. Well, the next job, of course, I'd shave it too fine, and maybe we'd be a nickel high. And I guess you know how he'd take that. I'd lost him a nice contract: if I'd had any sense, I'd have made the bid low enough to cinch the job.

So I'd been getting pretty jumpy and nervous. Not eating or sleeping much, and living mostly on coffee. I was about fit to be tied (and I still am). When he wasn't riding me, he was watching me, staring out into the outer office at the back of my neck. And I could just put up with it so long, and then my kidneys would start cutting up and I'd have to go back to the restroom. That's the way it always affects me when I get jumpy and nervous. I know it's just the opposite with some people—they get bound up, But, me, it gets my kidneys every time.

This day I'm telling you about, I'd been to the restroom three times in less than three hours. The third time I came back to my desk, Henley jerked his head at me. I went into his office, and maybe my knees weren't knocking together but they sure felt like it.

"What's the matter with you?" he said. Just like that.

"What do you mean, what's the matter?" I said. Honestly, I didn't know what to say, I was too rattled to think.

"What are you chasing all over the office for? Can't you stay out of that restroom for five minutes? How can you ever get any work done if you're never at your desk."

"I manage to get my work done," I said.

"I asked you a question." He scowled at me. "You must have been back to the toilet six times in the last half hour."

I knew there was no use correcting or arguing with him. I knew I'd better think of something fast or I'd be in big trouble. And it was just about the worst time possible for *that* kind of trouble. Mother—Martha's mother, that is—had been having some pretty hefty doctor bills, and it looked like Martha was going to need a new upper plate any day—it hadn't been much good since she'd got it mixed up with the garbage and put it in the incinerator—and Bob was just getting started in high school. Bob had gone right from the Kenton Hills Grammar School to Kenton Hills High School. He'd gone from grade to grade with the same kids, ever since he'd started to school, and I hated to think of how he'd feel if I lost my job and we had to move and he had to start into some strange school with a strange bunch of kids. He hadn't been doing too well in school lately, as it was. It might set him back seriously if he had to make a change now.

Henley was waiting for me to say something. He was hoping I'd tangle myself up, give him an excuse to fire me. I think he was, anyway.

"Well," he said, "how about it? For God's sake, are you deaf and dumb?"

And all of a sudden I had an inspiration.

"No, I'm not deaf and dumb," I said, looking him straight in the eye, "and I'm not blind either."

"Huh?" he grunted. "What do you mean?"

"I mean that restroom was getting to be a kind of play room," I said. "People have been hanging around back there, smoking and swapping jokes, when they should be out here working. I'm putting a stop to it."

"Well, say, now." He leaned back in his chair. "That's all right, Al! Been giving 'em hell, huh?"

"They get out fast," I said, "when they see me coming."

"Who were they, Al, some of the worst offenders? Give me their names."

"Well . . ." I hesitated. And I thought about Jeff Winter and Harry Ainslee and some of the others that had tried to knife me every time I turned my back. One of their favorite tricks was to loaf along until they saw I was tied up on something, then spring some deal that had to be settled right away. You know, trying to make it look like I was slowing down. Like I was a bottleneck and they couldn't get their jobs done on account of me.

But I wasn't going to be lowdown just because they were. I wouldn't be like them for any amount of money.

"I think one's been about as bad as another," I said. "I wouldn't want to name anyone in particular."

"Mmmm. Uh-huh," he nodded. "Well, I'll tell you what you'd better do, Al. You lock the place up, and keep the key at your desk. Make 'em come to you for it whenever they want to go."

So that's what I did. That's how I squeezed out of one of the tightest places I'd ever been in. And there wasn't anything wrong with it, was there? After all, I was supposed to be in charge of the outer office. The men should get permission from me before leaving their work.

Henley didn't ride me about a thing for the rest of the day, and he stopped watching me. Then that night, as I was getting ready to leave, he called me into his office again.

"Been thinking about you, Al," he said. "Looks like you're more on the ball than I thought you were. You keep it up, and maybe we can boost you to three-fifty."

"Why, that's—that's fine!" I said. My salary was three twenty-seven-fifty a month (and it still is). "I'll certainly do all I can to deserve it."

"Three-fifty," he said, his eyes veiled, smiling in a way I didn't understand. "That's pretty good money for a man your age, isn't it?"

"Well" I laughed. "I'm not exactly a Methuselah, Mr. Henley. I won't be forty-nine until next—"

"Yeah? You don't think it is good money?"

"Yes, sir. I mean—I was just going to say that. . . . Yes, sir," I said.

"You agree you'd be damned lucky to get it, a man your age?"

"I'd be . . . be darned lucky to get it," I said. "A man my age."

I went on home, not feeling too good although there wasn't any reason why I shouldn't have. I'd done the right thing, the only thing I could have done. I hadn't hurt anyone and it looked like I might have got myself a raise, so everything was all right. But I guess I kind of wanted someone to tell me it was.

We had pickled beets, peas, and sweet potatoes for dinner that night. It seemed that Martha had taken the labels off the cans to make some candlestick shades, and she didn't know what was in them until she opened them up.

I said it was a dandy dinner, the very things I liked. Sometimes I forget myself and scold her, but I try not to. She can't help it, you see, according to the doctors. She's been a little giddy ever since she started going through the change of life. Maybe even before.

Well, so we all started eating, and I brought up the matter of the raise in an offhand way. I mentioned that first, and then I just sort of dragged in the other things, the restroom and so on.

Martha said it was wonderful; she carried on for a minute or two about how smart I was. "I guess you showed them," she said. "They have to get up pretty early in the morning to get ahead of my Al."

Bob looked down at his plate, He didn't eat anything.

"Didn't you hear your father?" Martha frowned at him. "All those people have been picking on him, and now he's got *them* in hot water. And maybe he'll get a raise besides!"

"I'll bet he don't," said Bob.

"Well, now," I said. "I really didn't get the boys in any trouble. Nothing like it. I simply . . . What makes you think I won't, Bob?"

"Nothing," he mumbled. "I'm not hungry."

"You see?" I laughed. "You can't tell me, can you? If you don't have a reason for a statement, you shouldn't make it."

" 'Scuse me," he said. "I don't want anything more to eat."

He pushed back his chair, and started to get up.

I told him to stay right where he was.

"Al," said Martha, nervously. "If he doesn't want to eat—"

"I'm handling this," I said. "I'm still head of this family. He acts like I'd—he made a certain statement. Now, he can explain himself or he'll sit there and eat."

Bob hesitated, his head bowed over his plate. He picked up his fork and began to eat.

"I don't think I'm unreasonable," I said. "Why, my God, if I'd been willing to do the things that some people do, I wouldn't have to—to—worry about a job. I'd be sitting on easy street. I'll tell you something, young man: if you had just a few of my problems, things I never even mention, maybe you'd . . ."

I went on talking to him, trying to show him where he was wrong. And he was wrong. Like I say, I'm not unreasonable. I'm not like Henley. I wasn't just being ornery, trying to make him say something he didn't want to just because I was worried and sore at myself.

I'm not like that. I hadn't done anything to be ashamed of.

"You see, Bob?" I said. "Answer me!"

He didn't answer. He poked a bite of sweet potato into his mouth.

And then, suddenly, he choked and his face went white, and he started vomiting.

. . . That's when he really changed.

He was never quite the same boy after that.

allen talbert 2

Well, here we go again, and this time I'll try not to ramble all over the reservation.

I started out to tell you about that day, *the* day it happened. I'll pick up where I left off, with Bob walking me part way to the station.

We were about six blocks from the house, almost to the corner where Bob had to turn off toward school, when a car pulled in at the curb. Jack Eddleman leaned out the window, grinning at us.

"What do you say there, Talberts?" he called. "What do you think of the new buggy?"

"It looks all right," I said, bearing down a little on the *looks*. "Real estate business must be good these days."

"All business is good. It just depends on the men that are in it."

"Is that a fact?" I said.

"Got you that time, huh?" He let out a laugh, that jackass bray of his. "Hop in and I'll drive you to the station."

"No, thanks," I said. "I'm walking with my son."

"Keepin' an eye on him, huh?" He laughed again. "How you getting along with the girls these days, Bob? Been under any washing machines lately?"

Bob tried to smile. He ducked his head, and started to turn away. I told him to wait. I said I had something to say to Mr. Eddleman, and I wanted him to hear it.

Then, I stepped out to the curb, and I'm telling you: maybe that big redfaced loud-mouth had never been told off before, but he was then.

I . . . I wonder if you're like I am? I mean, sometimes I can speak up and lay down the law to people, and at others I'm just as mild as milk. I'll let them walk all over me. It seems like I just can't find the words or the nerve to say anything.

I remember when Martha and I were on our honeymoon. We'd taken a room American plan at this Niagara Falls hotel, and I'd had to pay in advance so, of course, we couldn't move. And, well, this head waiter in the dining room, he'd treated us like dirt right from the beginning. I don't know why. We'd tipped well, and we hadn't demanded any extra service or anything like that. I guess he just picked on us because he thought he could get away with it.

Well, he *did* get away with it for a while, three—no, four days. It was dinner of the fourth night when I jumped him. He'd set us down at a little table back near the kitchen, and the table cloth may have been white at one time, but you'd never have known it. There was enough catsup and gravy on it to paint a barn door.

"I'd like another table," I said, "or at least a clean cloth."

"No kidding," he said, real sarcastically. "You're pretty hard to please, aren't you?"

I kicked back my chair, and jumped up. I shoved my face right up against his. "You're doggone right, I'm hard to please," I said, "and I'm pretty hard to get along with when I'm not pleased, so maybe you'd better not give me any more trouble. Just a little more nonsense like you've been pulling"—I said—"and I'm liable to mop up the floor with you. Now, you give us a good table and make it fast, and from now on you watch your p's and q's when you're around us."

Well, he folded up like an accordion, didn't give me a word of back talk. He took us to the best table in the dining room, and for the next three days you'd have thought we were royalty, the service we got.

Martha couldn't get over the way I'd acted. She was as proud as punch of me, but it startled the daylights out of her.

"My goodness," she kept saying. "I never knew you could be like that, Al."

"Well, sometimes I can and sometimes I can't," I said. "I guess I take just so much, and then I blow up."

Well, as I was saying. Any other time, I might have let Jack Eddleman get away with it; I'd let him get away with a lot of stuff before this. But this time he was picking on the wrong party.

"Now, I'll tell you something, Jack," I said. "I don't think we'd better have any more talk about that washing machine business. Neither to me or Bob or anyone else. Your daughter came over to our house uninvited. She walked right in while Mrs. Talbert and I were away, and wandered out into the kitchen where Bob was working. If she'd minded her own business like he was minding his, there—"

"Oh, yeah?" He tried to look tough, but his eyes shifted. "It's a darned good thing I looked in your back door. If I hadn't've come over to borrow a hoe, that overgrown youngun of yours would have—well, I won't say it."

"I think you'd better," I said. "I want to hear you say it."

"Aw, hell . . ." He forced a laugh. "What are we arguing about? You know how I am. I just like to kid."

"Yes, I know how you are," I said. "I've had you sized up for a long time. You keep riding people, making 'em uncomfortable, and the longer they take it the rougher you get. Then, when they call you on it you say you're kidding."

"Huh!" he said. "Look who's talking."

"I don't care whether you look or not," I said, "but you'd better remember what I told you."

He slammed his car into gear, and drove off.

I turned around to Bob. His shoulders weren't sagging now, and he was really smiling instead of just trying to. He was looking at me like he'd used to, like he had that Monday morning in New York when Martha had been afraid I'd be late for work and I'd said Henley could go jump if he didn't like it.

"Gosh," he said. "Gol-lee, Dad. Thanks a lot!"

"It wasn't anything," I said. "I should have called the big bluffer a long time ago."

"I didn't mean that. Not just that. I mean the way you stuck up for me."

"I see," I said. "I—it's this way, Bob. I'm probably overly concerned about you, anxious to keep you out of trouble, and maybe it appears sometimes that I think you did something—that I'm accusing you—when I'm just trying to protect you. I never thought for a minute that there was anything wrong going on between you and Josie under that washing machine."

"Well, gosh," he said, scuffing the toe of his shoe against the sidewalk. "Darn that old girl, anyway."

"You don't have anything more to do with her, do you?" I said.

"Huh-uh. Not much of anything, anyway. I see her at school, of course, and sometimes a bunch of us will be over to the soda fountain together or something like that. But . . ."

"I'd be pretty careful around her," I said. "It's not that I don't trust you, but I've seen girls like Josie Eddleman before. They can get a boy into an awful lot of trouble."

"Sure, Dad," he said, kind of embarrassed. "I know."

He went on toward school, running to catch up with some other kids.

I went on to the railroad station, and caught the 8:05 into town.

We'd been neighbors with the Eddlemans for almost eleven years. They live at 2200 Canyon Drive, the far southeast corner overlooking the canyon, and we live at 2208 which is four doors down the street. At the time we moved here, there weren't any houses between theirs and ours, and we got to be pretty good friends. Bob was less than a year older than Josie, so naturally they played together, and Fay Eddleman was always trotting across the vacant lots to see Martha, or vice versa, and Jack and I saw quite a bit of each other.

It went on like that for a couple of years, and then a house went up between us and we weren't quite so thick any more. We couldn't be, you know, and frankly I was just as glad that we couldn't. I was glad when the other two vacant lots were built on, and we hardly ever saw Fay and Jack unless we ran into them on the street. They just weren't the kind of people who wore well. You never felt like you could hardly trust 'em. They were always running someone down—joking in a way that could hurt—and I figured that if they did that with other people they probably did it to us.

Of course, the kids went on seeing each other. Hardly a day passed that Bob wasn't over to Josie's house or Josie wasn't over to our place. After all, they'd practically grown up together, and there weren't any other children in our block.

By the time Bob was twelve or thirteen, he began to lose interest in Josie. He went over to her house less and less, and when she dropped in on us, he was just as likely as not to go off and leave her. He'd go up to the school grounds and play football or maybe he'd wander down to the canyon to play Tarzan with some other boys. Or sometimes he'd just go up to his room and stay until she left.

Martha scolded him about it, not being polite to a guest, and I spoke to him a time or two, but it didn't seem to have much effect. He went right on being indifferent and acting like she wasn't around, and I was pretty pleased that he did. The more he steered clear of Josie Eddleman, the better it suited me. I don't like to sound dirty-minded or suspicious, but that girl worried me. I've seen grown women who weren't nearly as well-developed as she was at twelve.

Well, one Saturday morning about four months ago, Martha and I walked up to the shopping center after groceries and Bob stayed at the house. There was a leak around the drain of the washing machine, and he was going to fix it. He was lying under the machine, fitting a new gasket he'd cut out of an old shoe, when Josie came in.

It was warm weather. She was wearing some kind of short pants called pedal-pushers and a floweredy thing they call a halter—but which is just a brassiere so far as I'm concerned—and that was all aside from some sandals. She hunkered down, watching him work. Pretty soon, almost before he knew what was happening, she'd crawled under the machine with him. He hadn't asked her to and he was getting along very well by himself, but she was going to give him some help.

Well, Martha and I came in on the tag end of the deal,

right after Jack had looked in the back door and started raising Cain, and Bob and Josie were on their feet by that time.
But I know it must have looked pretty bad, even though,
I'm sure, there wasn't anything in the way of monkey business. You take a big boy like Bob and a half-naked girl like
Josie and squeeze them together between the legs of a
washing machine, and it just doesn't look good.

I was pretty excited, I guess, and I didn't handle the matter very well. I bawled Bob out and sent him to his room,
and I suppose I said things to Jack that could be construed
as an apology. I guess I acted like there really was something wrong, and it was all Bob's fault.

No, I didn't handle it well. What I should have done was
to tell Jack to take that girl home and wallop her backside
and see that she stayed at home. At least see that she
stayed away from our house. He knew what she was like as
well as I did, He didn't want to admit it, but he knew it was
a pretty blamed good idea to keep an eye on her. That's
why he'd been over slipping around our back yard and
looking in our back door. He'd just made up that story
about wanting to borrow a hoe.

Well, anyway, I'd told him off this morning, and it wasn't
as good doing it now as it would have been at the time, but
better late than never. Bob had been pleased as could be. I
felt pretty good about it.

It looked like I was going to have a mighty fine day, with
the start I'd gotten, and I did have a fine one. Right up until
the last of it, that is.

I'd been at work about an hour when a woman phoned in
with a complaint. The call went to Henley first. Apparently,
she was a little too hot for him to handle, so he switched
her to me but stayed in on the line.

A lot of the tiles in her bathroom were turning brown.
Since it was our sub-contract, she wanted us to do the job
over. In fact, she was darned well going to make us do it
over or take us into court.

"A brand-new house," she kept saying. "A brand-new
bathroom and already it looks like some old privy!"

Well, naturally, we weren't going to re-tile the place.

There just isn't any profit in residential work, as it is. People only have so much money to spend, but they insist on having all kinds of tile. If they were smart, they'd take less and get a better job. But they just won't do that; they just won't understand that you can't get something for nothing.

A tile contractor comes along, say, and he says, Why, yes, lady (or mister), I can give you a five-foot border there on the walls and I'll give you a three-color terrazzo mosaic for the floor, and I'll keep the job under three hundred. Then, you come along and you say, Why, no, I couldn't do that; I'd have to substitute quantity for quality. But I can give you a *first-class* four-foot border and a *first-class* plain block floor for three hundred. And you know who will get the job. They'll pick the first man every time.

So you have to cut corners, if you want to stay in business. You use cheaper materials and you push the men as hard as they'll be pushed, and whenever the union will let you get away with it you sneak in apprentices instead of using journeymen. Naturally, the work won't hold up, although some jobs hold up longer than others. It just isn't quality.

I let this woman rave on a while, working the mad out of her system, and finally I cut in on her.

"I wanted to ask you, madam," I said. "Were you out around the job any while the house was being built? Well, did you notice whether any of the plasterers were chewing tobacco?"

"Why . . . well, yes," she said. "What's that got to do with it?"

"Tile is highly absorbent," I explained. "It has a suction action on anything it comes into contact with. If you happen to have one left over from the job you can prove it to yourself. Put the back of it down in some coffee grounds, say. Before long a brown stain will show through the glaze. Now, I imagine one of the plasterers must have spit into his mortar and . . ."

The majority—well, at least a lot—of plasterers do chew tobacco. It's hard for them to smoke in their line of work, so they chew instead. And the way most women feel about chewing tobacco, and the men who chew it, it was easy for this one to believe that her gripe was against the plastering contractor rather than us.

She wouldn't get any satisfaction out of him, of course. No plasterer in his right mind would spit tobacco juice into his mortar, and they aren't paying crazy men thirty dollars a day. But I'd got her off our backs.

I hung up the receiver, turning around to look at Henley as he hung up his.

He grinned and waved his hand at me.

Early that afternoon, as soon as I got the routine stuff out of the way, I unlocked the private file and took out the drawings—the blueprints—on the new city stadium. We weren't supposed to have detail drawings, naturally, until the job was put up for bid. But one of the draftsmen in the architect's office had sneaked us out a set for a hundred and fifty dollars.

I went over them carefully, like I'd been going over them for the past ten days, trying to figure out a way of using the edge they gave us. Finally, along around quitting time, I found it.

I carried the drawings in to Henley's office and spread them out in front of him.

"I've been studying these tunnels," I said, tracing them out with a pencil. "They're going to be subjected to unusually heavy wear. I think they ought to have something unusually durable in the way of tile."

"Yeah?" He shrugged irritably. "The architect don't think so. Wouldn't cut much ice for us if he did."

"Unusually durable," I repeated, giving him a slow wink. "An extra-heavy imported Italian."

"Yeah, but . . ." His eyes widened suddenly, and he let out a grunt. Then he leaned back in his chair, pursing out his lips, "Uh-*huh*," he said. "Were you thinking about a certain tile that a certain contractor named Henley got stuck with, that he's got almost a warehouse full of? Stuff that the government cancelled out on because a lighter tile does the job just as good?"

"That's it," I said. "I was thinking that outside of our

supply there probably isn't a hundred square feet of it in the country."

"By George!" He slapped his hand down on the desk. "I doubt like hell that you can get it anywhere. They just don't make it any more. If we could get that written into the specifications . . ."

"I don't think we can," I said. "We'd have to work through the building department. Get them to write a proviso into the code to fit the situation. No one could kick about it. It's an unusual type of building and the code could logically be amended to take care of it."

"Yeah, I guess we could get away with it all right. But that building department! It really costs when you buy something from those boys."

"What's the difference?" I said. "If no one else can bid on the job, we can set our own price."

"Well, by God!" he said. "We can. Al, this calls for a drink!"

He made me sit down, and got a bottle out of his desk. We sat there drinking and talking until quitting time.

"You know, Al," he said. "You know what I'm going to do if this goes over all right? I'm going to re-tile the bathroom for that woman who called this morning."

"I'll bet she'd appreciate it," I said.

"Here's the way I see it," he went on. "There's no percentage in this penny ante stuff, keeping people locked out of the restroom or chiseling someone on a two-by-four residential job. You're worried and you figure everyone's out to do you so you do them first. But it does something to you, know what I mean? You lose more than you make."

"I guess you're right about that," I said.

"Unlock that damned restroom tomorrow, will you? Throw the key away. Why, good God, Al, what are we coming to when a man has to get permission to go to the toilet? It's cheap, degrading. A man who would put up with it long isn't worth having. I don't know why in the world I ever . . ."

He shook his head, pausing to pour us a drink. He looked up at me, and shook his head again.

"You know what I always liked about you, Al? Character. A man may not have too much of it himself, but he likes to see it in other people. Yes, sir, that was it, Al. Character. The guts to stand up and speak out. I liked that."

"Well, thanks very much," I said. "I guess none of us is everything we should be, but I do the best I can. By the way, I was going to ask if—uh—about that raise . . ."

"Character. It's something you don't find very often, Al, and when you lose it it's gone for good. You're just one more animal in the herd. . . . Raise?"

"We were talking about it a while back," I said. "Putting me up to three-fifty. I don't want any credit for doing what I'm paid to do—doing my job—but I did think of the angle on this city stadium deal and—"

"I'm giving you credit for it, Al. Full credit," he said. "We'll keep thinking about the raise."

It was after five, and everyone but us had left. I let him out of the office, and then I locked up and started home.

All and all, it had been a good day.

Pretty good, that is.

martha talbert 3

Well, actually! I honestly thought I was going to fly to pieces. The one morning when I simply couldn't let myself get unnerved.

I was hoping I could get Al out of the house before Bob came down, and I did everything but shove him out the door. But, no, it was no use. He had to choose that morning to take his time, and Bob had to choose that one to hurry. So they were both at the breakfast table at the same time, and goodness! I can't tell you what it did to my nerves. It's bad enough at other meals, but breakfast—honestly! I thought I was going to go crazy. And me in my change of life.

They seemed to be getting along all right, but I knew it couldn't last. I knew that, sooner or later, Al would say something sharp to Bob and Bob would say something back, or he wouldn't say anything which always makes Al worse than when Bob *does* say something. So I waited for it to happen. I hovered around them, smiling and trying to talk, and generally acting like a Gonmolian idiot or whatever you call them. I wished it would happen so they could just get it over with and I wouldn't have to wait any more. I actually think sometimes that the waiting is worse than the other.

Well, they finally finished breakfast, thank goodness, and if they'd taken another five minutes I'd have been in hysterics. Al asked me if I was feeling well when he kissed me good-bye, and Bob said, "Gee, Mom, why don't you lie down a while." And I don't remember what I said, but it was probably something silly. I felt like a balloon, all swelled up and getting bigger and bigger every moment. I thought I was going to explode.

They went off down the street together, talking just as pleasantly as you please, and I could feel the blood rushing into my face and I felt like I was choking. I don't think I've ever been so angry in my life. I'll tell you, if I could have got my hands on those two right then I'd've shook 'em until their teeth rattled. I mean, well, here they'd put me through all that strain and then they hadn't done anything! They'd—they'd—oh, well! What's the use talking about it?

I peeked out through the living room drapes, watching them until they were out of sight, and then I just fell down on the lounge and started bawling. Actually. You'd have thought I'd been killed the way I was bawling. So finally I looked up into the hall mirror and my eyes were all red and my nose looked like a tomato or something, and I stopped crying and began to laugh. And then I felt a lot better.

I went out into the kitchen and had a cup of coffee. I started to fix myself a bite of breakfast, because I was feeling a little hungry now, and right away I broke a whole dozen eggs.

I don't know why Al does things like that. For a man who's supposed to be smart, and of course he is smart, he can do some of the foolishest things. Now, he knows that I always put the egg carton right on the edge of the top refrigerator shelf. That way, you know, I know it won't take much for them to fall out, so I watch them to see that they won't fall out. But what does he do but come along and stick them way back to the rear on the bottom shelf; and naturally I can't imagine what in the world. I can't see them anywhere. So I began pulling shelves out, right and left, and oops! there went the eggs. All over the floor.

I don't know why Al does those things.

Fortunately, I'd mopped late the night before, so I scraped the eggs up into a bowl and got the shells out of them. I felt quite well by the time I'd finished. It always makes me feel better to break something, and this solved the dinner problem. We'd just have a nice dish of scrambled eggs.

I had a piece of toast and some more coffee, and got dressed. I took another look at the letter from Miss Brundage, and then I tore it up and flushed it down the toilet. Miss Brundage was Bob's homeroom teacher, and it seemed to me that if she did her job and minded her own business she wouldn't have so much time to write letters to parents. Naturally, I didn't tell Al about the letter. He fusses at Bob enough as it is. And I didn't say anything to Bob about it. It wasn't necessary. If a mother doesn't know her own son, who does? Some teacher, a *miss*? Someone that's never had a child in her life?

Well, of course, she may have had some for all I know. She probably should have had some. These women that go on year after year, staying single and dodging their responsibilities and putting almost everything they make on their backs, well, I've got some ideas about them. They may think they're fooling people, but they don't fool me.

I'm not saying she is that way, mind you. I don't believe in making judgments on people until I know all the facts. But it certainly seems strange.

Anyway, people that are always so anxious to criticize someone else shouldn't complain when people criticize them.

Judge not lest you be judged, I always say.

Well, I wore my black and green plaid and that yellow short coat and I guess it does make me look like a checkerboard inside of a banana skin, but I just couldn't help it. I imagine I look quite as well as most women my age. As long as you're clean and neat and respectable, that's what counts.

I don't know why in the world I ever bought the darned things.

So, finally, I left the house, and I don't know yet how I made it after everything that had happened to me. But I did though—what a morning!—and of course the first thing I saw was Fay Eddleman out on the walk in front of their place.

Honestly. I don't know why she just doesn't set up a tent out there and live in it. I don't know how she ever gets her housework done. Why, I've watched her all morning or all afternoon sometimes, just to see if she ever did go in. And she never did. She'd just go in to eat or something, and then she'd rush right back out again. I've watched her, and I know.

First the milkman comes by, and he has to stop and talk. And then it's the bakeryman and the mailman and the garbage man, and, oh, I don't know what all. Anything that wears pants. And they can't get away from her. She'll stand there and she'll talk and she'll talk, and I wouldn't want to say anything definite but I just wish I could read lips sometimes. Anyone that acts like she does, there's something funny going on.

If the weather isn't forty below zero or something, she'll wear some kind of shorts or slacks, just as tight as she can get 'em. And those sweaters she wears: I think she must have to grease herself to get them on. But whatever she's wearing, it doesn't make much difference. She still doesn't look like she had anything on.

She knows it, too, and don't you think she doesn't! It's deliberate.

She'll stand out there with that reddish brown hair blowing all over her face (naturally, it's hennaed, the hair I mean) and she'll look up at someone—a man, of course—with those reddish brown eyes, and she'll say something and then she'll wiggle. Giggle and wiggle all over. She'll pull her chin down into her bosom (and she doesn't have to pull it very far, believe me) and she'll roll her eyes up at this man and say something. And then he'll say something, and she'll wiggle. Wiggle and giggle. And it actually makes you blush to watch her.

Well, she waited until I was almost on top of her, and then she acted like she'd just then seen me.

"Why, Martha!" she said. "Of all things, darling! Where in the world have you been keeping yourself?"

I pretended like I'd just seen her, too.

"Goodness!" I said. "Is that really you, Fay? Oh, I've just been busy around the house. You know how it is when you have to take care of a family."

"Yeah," she said. "Don't I though!"

"It doesn't leave you much time for yourself," I said. "I don't think I've been out of the house in weeks."

"You should get out more, Martha," she said. "I think it ages a woman to stick in the house all the time."

"I suppose it does," I said, "but if a woman is a woman, why shouldn't she look like one? I think there's nothing more ridiculous than to see some middle-aged woman trying to get herself up like a teen-ager."

I smiled at her, staring right at the front of that overstuffed sweater and then taking a slow look down at those skin tight slacks.

"That reminds me," I said, "I've simply got to get some new washing powder. The one I'm using just shrinks everything I have."

"But, darling!" she said. "You don't mean you've been washing that perfectly adorable dress! And here I thought you'd just put on a little weight."

She smiled at me, staring at my dress as though she'd never seen one before.

I could understand that, naturally. It'd been so long since she wore a dress that she'd forgotten what they looked like.

"Were you going up to the school?" she said. "I *do* hope Bob isn't in trouble again."

"Trouble?" I said. "No, that's the advantage of having a

boy. You never have any trouble with them. I'm just walking up to the shopping center for a while."

"I'll bet you're going to get a permanent," she said. "Why don't you wait until it gets cold, Martha? Perhaps your hair will thicken up, then, and it'll take better."

"No, I don't think I'll get any more permanents," I said. "You go in those places and you get the same operators who've been dyeing some old bag's hair, and then they go right to work on you. Like the last time, remember? No, I guess we didn't go together; you were leaving the shop just as I came in. Anyway, they'd just finished dyeing this woman's hair, whoever she was, and I got the same operator. And my goodness, Fay! Stink! It took me days to get that awful smell out of my hair."

"I suppose it's all in what you're used to," she said. "I remember we had an old Negro woman working for us years ago, so naturally she used a black dye. And do you know, Martha? She couldn't stand the smell of red—of any other color."

"Well," I said, "I guess I'd better be getting along. It was certainly nice to see you again, Fay."

"You haven't seen anything of Josie, have you?" she said. "She had a sore throat so I let her stay home from school today, and the minute I turn my back she chases off somewhere."

"Oh, that's terrible," I said. "She's liable to get pneumonia running around without any clothes on."

"She's got clothes on"— Fay got a little red in the face. "A kid doesn't need to be bundled up like an Eskimo on a nice fall day."

"Well, I'd be awfully careful with her," I said. "A person with a large—uh—chest like that, they catch pneumonia very easily."

"Why didn't Bob go to school today?" she said. "I wonder if he could have seen anything of Josie."

"Bob did go to school today," I said. "And I'm quite sure he wouldn't have seen anything of Josie if he hadn't gone."

"Well, he didn't pass by here," she said. "I'm sure I couldn't have missed him."

"He went the other way," I said, "like he used to. He wanted to walk part way to the train with his father."

"Well, I kind of wondered," she said. "I caught a glimpse of someone down in the canyon a while ago in a blue and white jacket."

"There's lots of blue and white jackets," I said.

She shook her head, absently, peering up and down the street.

"That girl," she said. "Now, where could she have gone to?"

I started to give her some ideas on the subject, but, oh, well. When someone's worried about a child, you just don't do those things.

"Maybe she decided to go on to school after all," I said. "Do you suppose she'd've done that, just gone on without saying anything?"

"Well, now, I'll bet that's just what she did," Fay said, "She must have. And here I've been worrying my head off about her."

"Why don't you call the school and make sure?" I said.

"Oh, I guess I won't," she said. "I'm sure she went, the darned crazy kid! She'd be mad if I called there and had them check on her. She'd say, Why, mother, you ought to've known, and so on. And she probably wouldn't speak to me for the next week."

"I know what you mean," I said. "I know exactly what you mean, Fay. You do or say some little thing around Bob—just doing what a parent should do, you know—and he acts like you're public enemy number one or something."

"I'll tell you, Martha," she said. "If I'd cut up and talked back to *my* mother, like Josie does to—"

"And *my* mother," I said. "Why, Fay, it just simply never would have occurred to me to behave around my mother like Bob—"

"Martha," she said, "what about some coffee? I've got some of those nice fresh pecan rolls you always used to like so much."

"Why I'd love to," I said.

Well, I went in, and we had coffee and rolls and a nice

little talk. Fay *can* be a very nice person when she wants to, and I'd be the first to admit it.

It was almost noon before I remembered that I was supposed to have seen Miss Brundage at eleven.

I jumped up and said I simply had to go, and Fay said, oh, why didn't I let the shopping go until tomorrow. But I guess she knew where I was really going, so she just argued enough to be polite. As I say, Fay *can* be nice.

I hurried on toward the school, and even if I was late for my appointment I can't say when I've felt so good. You wouldn't have thought I was the same woman that had been all fly-to-pieces a couple of hours ago.

It's like that with me. Bad beginning, good ending. Foul start, fine finish.

It's almost always like that with me.

martha talbert 4

I reached the school just as the noon bells were ringing, and if I didn't look a fright it wasn't my fault. I'd practically galloped every step of the way from Fay's house because there's just no sense in people being late for appointments, and I never am when I can possibly avoid it. Well, as I was saying, I know I must have looked a fright what with all that running and then having to climb three flights of stairs and squeezing past eight or nine hundred kids who were trying to beat each other to the cafeteria, but that certainly didn't give Miss Brundage any right to act like I was something the cat dragged in. She was coming out of her classroom—Bob's home room—as I started in, and she kept right on coming out. Barely nodding to me, kind of pushing me out of her way.

"I'm very sorry you couldn't keep our appointment, Mrs. Talbert," she said. "I'm afraid that, unless you can wait until after three . . ."

"Wait until after three!" I said. "Why, of course, I can't."

"Perhaps we'd better make it tomorrow, then. Between eleven and twelve. I believe I explained—didn't I?—that it was the only hour of the day I had free."

"Well, of all things!" I said. "You're free now, aren't you? You don't have anything to do now that I can see!"

"Yes," she said. "I do have something to do now. I have to eat my lunch."

She gave me a cool little nod and started down the hall and, honestly, it was all I could do not to grab her and shake her right out of her dress. Really, you know, you'd have thought she was the president of the United States or something and I was I-don't-know-what. And just what was all the fuss about, pray tell? It was my lunch hour, too, wasn't it? I hadn't had any lunch yet, either, and you didn't see me acting like the world was going to come to an end if I didn't eat right that minute.

"Now, just a minute, Miss Brundage," I said, and I ran and caught up with her. "If you *please*, Miss Brundage! You asked me to come here today, and I came, and now that I'm here I'm—"

"Our appointment was at eleven, Mrs. Talbert. I'm sure I explained—"

"Well, I couldn't get here at eleven," I said. "I got here just as fast as I could and I almost broke my neck doing it. I thought it was something very, very important the way you acted, and if I'd known it wasn't anything that really mattered, that you didn't want to bother with until you could take your own sweet time about it—well, believe me I had plenty of other things I could do. I'm not like some of you young girls with nothing to think about but getting your lunch on time and how you can doll yourselves all up like the president of the United States or something. I tell you teachers weren't like that, in my day. They knew how to handle their jobs, and they weren't always calling parents up every five minutes and writing notes and . . ."

I laid it into her. I told that young lady a few things she'd be a long time forgetting.

She stood staring at me, her mouth opening and closing, her face getting redder and redder.

"All right," she said finally, her voice so low I could hardly hear it. "I'll be very happy to talk to you now. I have a feeling that, in view of your opinion of me, there isn't a great deal to be said, but—"

"Go on," I said. "What's Bob supposed to have done now?"

"It's more what he hasn't done, Mrs. Talbert. He's done almost no work since the term started. He's failing in every one of his subjects."

"Why, I—well, why do you let him?" I said. "He's a smart boy. Why don't you see that he studies?"

"Mrs. Talbert," she said, "the teachers in this school have an average class load of sixty students, approximately twice the number they should have. We can't spend all our time with one pupil or even a very large part of our time."

"Well, goodness," I said. "No one asked you to. You don't have to, if you know your business. Why, when I was in school, there was only one teacher for six grades and she—"

"No doubt," she said. "I'm sure she was much more efficient than we teachers are now. To get back to the present, however, Robert is failing in his work and we don't seem to be able to help him. We wondered whether there wasn't something you and Mr. Talbert could do."

"Well, I don't know," I said. "We'll certainly do anything we can, I'll give Bob a good talking to, and—"

"He seems to be very preoccupied and moody. Is there—uh—a situation at home which might tend to disturb him?"

"Why, of course, there isn't!" I said. "If there's anything wrong anywhere, it's right here at school. And if you ask me, you don't have to look very far to see what it is."

She pressed her lips together. "Mrs. Talbert," she said. "I'm only trying to help—"

"Well, don't trouble yourself," I said. "We don't need any advice about how to run our family. What else is Bob supposed to have done?"

"He's supposed," she said, "to attend school five days a week. Five days, Mrs. Talbert. Not two or three."

"Well," I said, "he does, doesn't he? I mean, I know he's been sick a lot, but—"

"He has been sick, then, Mrs. Talbert?" There was a mean, funny little grin on her face. "You did write the excuses he brought us?"

"Why—well, naturally," I said. "When he's sick and has to stay at home, I write an excuse."

"I see," she said, that little grin getting meaner and tighter. "Well, why don't we do this, Mrs. Talbert? Why don't you and I and Bob all get together and see if we can't talk this thing out?"

I said that suited me just fine, the sooner the better. "Of course, I wouldn't think of asking you to miss your lunch, Miss Brundage. But—"

"I've already missed it," she said, "I'm afraid it's too late to eat now. So if you'd like to telephone home, and summon Robert from his sickbed, perhaps we can talk a few minutes before my afternoon classes start."

I didn't understand what she meant for a moment. It simply hadn't occurred to me that Bob hadn't gone to school, and the way she'd led me on, tricking me into making a fool of myself, well, I felt like choking her.

"Well?" she said. "Would you like to do that, Mrs. Talbert?"

"No," I said, and believe me if looks could have killed, that young woman would have been dead. "No, I would not like to do that, Miss Brundage. But there's something I would like to do. I'd like to know why we have to pay big taxes without getting anything for it but some snotty young girl to insult us. I'd like to know why we can't get teachers who think about something besides powdering their noses and putting every nickel they make on their backs and—"

"Mrs. Talbert," she said. "*Mrs. Talbert!*"

"Well, what?" I said. "You don't need to yell at me!"

"I'm a teacher, Mrs. Talbert, not a prison warden. I can't compel Robert to study and I can't keep him from playing truant. But I can—and I will, if you persist in your present attitude—I can and will see that action is taken by the proper authorities."

"Well, well," I said. "Now, let me tell you something Miss High-and-mighty. My husband and I—"

"There are compulsory attendance laws in this state, Mrs. Talbert. A parent who willfully allows a child to remain out of school is subject to heavy penalties."

"And wouldn't you love that!" I said.

"Yes," she nodded slowly. "I believe I would."

She turned and walked away, then, and it was a good thing for her that she did! I started after her, but then I thought, oh, well, what's the use? Anyone like that, it's a waste of breath to talk to 'em.

I left the school and walked back to the shopping center. I tried on a few pair of shoes and two coats and several hats, and got a book from the lending library. Then, I went into the drug store and ordered some pie and a cup of coffee. I wasn't at all hungry, really, even though I hadn't had hardly a bite to eat all day. But the lady sitting next to me, she was having an olive-nut triple-deck with cream cheese and it looked so good, I decided to have one, too. And somehow this lady and I got to talking—she was telling me about a perfectly marvelous diet she'd been on—and we had some more coffee and a chocolate sundae apiece, and the first thing we knew, it was almost three o'clock.

I started home, getting some milk and bread from the grocery first. I was almost there when, lo and behold, who should pop up in front of me suddenly but Mr. Bob Talbert. We saw each other at the same time, and did that young man look sheepish! Then, he put on a grin and tried to act like he was just getting home from school.

"Hi, Mom," he said. "Let me carry that stuff for you."

"Oh, I wouldn't think of it," I said. "After all, you've been studying all day, bending over your books until you're all worn out. You—oh, Bob, how could you? Aren't you ever going to straighten up and behave like a boy should?"

"I'm sorry," he mumbled. "I won't do it any more, Mom."

"Well, I should hope not!" I said. "Where on earth did you go anyway? Where have you been?"

"Out to the golf links. I was going to caddy—g-get some money to buy Dad a present."

I looked at him. Honestly, you know! Sometimes you'd think that boy didn't have a brain in his head. "Buy him a present?" I said. "What in the world for? It's not his birthday or anything."

"I just wanted to," he muttered. "I don't know why."

"Well, you certainly put me in a pretty pickle," I said. "I went up to see your teacher, and naturally I supposed you were there—what in the world would I be supposed to suppose?—and she and I started going around and around and—"

"Aw, Mom," he said. "For gosh sake, what'd you do that for? She's—Miss Brundage's the only one up there that's got any sense or ever acts half-way decent and you have to—"

"Well, for pity's sake!" I said. "You make a fool out of me with your hooky-playing, and then it's my fault. *I'm* in the wrong!"

"Well, gosh," he said. "Gee whiz, Mom!"

I told him he'd *better* gosh and gee-whiz. And he'd better start studying and stop playing truant or he'd wish he had. "The idea, just wandering off wherever you please and whenever you please! Did you make any money?"

"Huh-uh." He shook his head without looking at me. "Too many other caddies around. Not enough people playing."

"Well, that's nice, isn't it?" I said, "You lay out of school all day and walk eight or ten miles, just as if shoe leather didn't cost anything, and you don't have a nickel to show for it. That's certainly smart, that is!"

"Well, all right!" he said. "All *right*! I said I wouldn't do it any more, didn't I?"

"You just bet you won't," I said. "Now hush up that yelling before Mrs. Eddleman hears you. Hush up and act like you've got some sense for a change."

Fay was out in front of her house, of course. When was she ever any other place? She said, "Hi, Martha, Bob. Did you see Josie at school today, Bob?"

"Huh?" Bob stared at her like a big goop, like he wanted her to know he'd been playing hooky. "What'd you say, Miz Eddleman?"

"I asked you if you'd seen Jo—"

"The cat's got his tongue, Fay," I laughed. "He always gets that way whenever anyone mentions Josie. He saw her all right. I just got through asking him myself."

"Aren't kids funny?" Fay laughed, too. "Well, I guess she'll be along pretty soon. It's still early yet."

Bob and I went on home. I knew he must be half-starved, so I told him to run up and wash real quick and I'd fix him a sandwich and a glass of milk.

"I'm not very hungry," he said. "I'd just as soon wait until dinner time. I—I think I'll take a bath, Mom."

"Bath?" I said. "Are my ears deceiving me? You're going to take a bath without being . . . Bob," I said, "come here a minute. What's that—what in the world have you got on the front of your pants?"

"Nothin'," he mumbled, kind of putting his hands in front of himself. "I just, well, I was straddling a fence on the way to the golf course, and I guess I must have scratched myself a little."

"Well, I should think you did!" I said. "Now, those pants will have to go to the cleaners and you've probably got blood all over your underwear, and—"

It was just too much for one day. You know, a person can just take so much and that's all they can take. I sat down on the lounge and began to bawl.

"Please, Mom," he said. "I'm sorry, and I p-promise I won't—"

"Oh, go on," I said. "Go on and get your bath, and be sure you soak good and use plenty of hot water. We'll be lucky if you don't get lockjaw."

He went on up the stairs and pretty soon I heard water running in the tub. I closed my eyes and lay back, listening to it, and it was kind of peaceful, and I guess I must have been extremely tired because the first thing I knew I'd gone to sleep. I mean, I didn't know it when I went to sleep, of course, but when I woke up I knew I'd been asleep.

It was practically dark, I'd been asleep for more than two hours.

I could hear Bob moving around in the bathroom; he was

still up there after all this time. And that was all wrong, of course: you'd have to know Bob to know how crazy it was. But there was something else wrong, too.

I could feel it inside of me, and it made me all sick and kind of shaky. I went to the door—it was like something was drawing me to it—and stepped out on the porch.

Fay Eddleman was out on her walk, and Jack, her husband, was there, too. He had his arms around her, and you couldn't see her face, just his, and it was as white as a sheet. He looked as sick as I felt. There were a couple of other men standing off a little to one side, policemen I guessed, though they didn't have on uniforms. And there was a police car drawn up at the curb. I thought, now, what in the world, but I didn't really wonder. Somehow I knew what was wrong, not exactly, you know, but close enough. I stood and looked at them, and finally I made myself look away. I turned and looked up the street, and I saw Al coming.

He was walking so slow, like he hated every step he took, so I guess he must have known, too.

One of the policemen said something to Jack, and he glanced up and nodded. Then, they started down the walk toward Al.

robert talbert　5

I don't know why. Why does everyone always want to know why, anyway? Gosh, if you always stop to wonder why every time you turn around you never get anything done. All I know is that I wanted to buy him a present, so instead of going on to school I cut back to the canyon and started for the golf course. That was all there was to it.

I went down the side of the canyon, and walked up that little creek that runs right through the center of it until I came to the railroad trestle. Then, I reached up and got ahold of a brace and started to swing across. Well, it wasn't my fault because, heck, I reckon I must have done the same thing a hundred times, and I bet I could do it in my sleep if I had to. But some way or another—well, maybe the dew had made it slick—my hand slipped; and I threw myself back real fast, but one foot went into the water clear up to my ankle.

Well, I kind of cussed, and then I laughed about it, because the way I was feeling, it would take a lot more than that to make me sore. Dad had been so nice and everything, and I was going to buy him a nice little present. And if everything went all right, well, I'd kind of have a little talk with him like we'd used to have. I'd get all the load off my mind about laying out of school and everything else I'd been doing, and he'd say, well, son, it's never too late to turn over a new leaf and I know you're going to do better from now on, and . . . Well, that's the way it would be. I could get out from under that load, and, boy, it was a *load!*

I took my shoe off, and shook the water out of it. Then, I wrung my sock out and hung it up on a bush to dry. I had plenty of time. I could make it to the golf course in an hour, easy; get in twenty-seven or maybe thirty-six holes if I got the breaks.

I hoped this wouldn't be one of those crummy days when there were maybe eighty-four caddies for every bag, and I thought, by gosh, it better not be. Not today, by golly. But I was feeling too good to worry about it.

I lay back on my back with my eyes closed, kind of daydreaming about how I was going to do and how things were going to be from now on. And I thought I heard something behind me, a kind of rustling and a twig cracking now and then, but I didn't pay any attention to it. I didn't have any idea she was within a million miles of me until she started running her fingers through my hair.

I jumped and sat up. She laughed, her head kind of cocked on one side. She was right up against me, almost; stooped down on her knees. I had to move away before I could sit up good.

"What the heck are you doing here?" I said. "Why aren't you in school?"

"I've got a cold," she said. "Why aren't *you* in school?"

"I suppose you're going to tell," I said. "Well, go ahead and see if I care."

"Huh-uh." She shook her head. "I wouldn't tell on you, Bobbie, no matter what you did."

"Well, go ahead," I said. "It don't make any difference to me what you do."

I reached up and got my sock off the bush. It felt pretty dry, so I started to put it on. She took it out of my hand—not snatching, or anything, but just sort of gentle and natural like—and hung it back up again.

"You want to catch cold, mmm?" she said. "Now, you just leave that right there until I tell you to put it on."

"Aw, heck," I said. "What do you care? Who asked you to come down here tellin' me what to do?"

"Well, it's a very good thing for you, I did," she said. "You certainly need someone to look after you."

I said she was crazy, just about a hundred times crazier'n any two people in the whole world. "I'll bet your mother doesn't know where you are. I'll bet you slipped off without telling her anything."

"I'll bet she doesn't know I copped her cigarettes, either," she nodded. "You want a cigarette, Bobbie?"

She had on some kind of funny looking shorts, not real short, you know, but the kind girls wear to ride bicycles and stuff like that. She had on that—them—and one of those tight goofy-looking blouses like her mother's always wearing, and a little button-up sweater that was kind of like her mother's, too. She had the sweater hung around her shoulders, instead of wearing it like anyone with some sense would, and the sleeves kept getting in the way when she tried to get the cigarettes and matches out of her blouse pockets.

"Well, Bobbie!" she said, finally, kind of pouting like it was my fault. "Aren't you going to help me?" So I said she was crazy again, but I got the stuff out of her pockets and she sort of stuck herself out so I could get to 'em, and gosh. I mean, well, it was the craziest feeling, me fumbling around in that goofy-looking blouse and her all arched out at me and—and everything.

I took a cigarette and she took one, and I held a match for us. I threw the cigarettes and matches back in her lap.

"Well," I said, "I got to be moving on pretty quick. I've got plenty of things to do today."

"Mmm?" she said, settling back on one elbow.

"Going out to the golf links," I said. "Pick myself up a few fast bucks."

"Mmm?" she blew out smoke, lazy-like. "So that's where you go when you play hooky so much."

"I don't always," I said. "I get a few bucks ahead, I go into town. I saved up almost ten bucks once, and boy did I have myself a time! I ate lunch there in the station restaurant and then I went to the penny arcade and a shooting gallery and another restaurant and all to heck around."

"Mmm," she said, "you awful bad boy, you."

"Well, heck," I said. "It doesn't sound like much fun, but it was."

She squeezed her cigarette out and lay back, one arm folded under her head. She smiled at me and kind of patted the ground at her side, so I lay back, too. It was a lot more comfortable that way, and I guess I'd kind of been wanting to see her. I guess I'd kind of missed her. I don't mean I *liked* her or anything like that, but you get used to someone, they're always around and then suddenly they aren't, and you can't help missing them.

We just sort of lay there, and, well, somehow or another her hand was in mine, but it didn't mean anything. I mean, it really didn't. Why, gosh, she'd always been tagging around after me as far back as I could remember and I'd hold onto her hand to keep her from falling or to help her over something, and maybe we hadn't held hands in a long time, but it seemed natural enough, like it ought to be, you know. Just there by ourselves, lying there and talking, it was all right.

"Bobbie . . ." she said.

"Yeah?" I said.

"Do you remember how we used to play together all day and then when I had to go home or you had to go home, we'd . . . we'd kiss each other good-bye."

"Heck," I said. "Yeah, I guess so."

"How long ago has it been, Bobbie? Since you kissed me."

"How do I know?" I said. "For gosh sake, Josie!"

"Well," she said. "If you're going to get mad every time I say anything, maybe I'd better go."

"Go ahead," I said. "You're the one that's mad. All I said was I didn't remember."

"You are too mad," she said. "I can always tell when you are."

"And I guess I don't know when I am," I said. "That's pretty rich, that is."

"You can't look me in the eye and say you're not mad," she said.

"I could if I wanted to," I said. "For gosh sake, Josie, why do you got to keep jabbering and fussing about—"

"You can't do it," she said. "I dare you to."

Well, I wasn't taking any dare from her, not any crazy old girl like that. So I rolled over, sort of, and looked at her and said I wasn't mad. I said it a couple of times, looking right at her, almost, but of course that wasn't good enough for her.

"You're mad all right," she said. "I can tell. If you weren't, well, you know what you'd do."

"For gosh sake, Josie," I said.

"Well, you would," she said. "Oh, B-Bobbie, what's the matter w-with—"

And, then, I hadn't done a darned thing, not a doggone thing, but she began to cry. She kind of cried, but not too much, and she sort of held her arms out, so, well, you know. I kissed her, and she kissed me, and she kept her arms around me when I started to move away.

I could feel her like I had when I'd got the cigarettes and matches, only I felt her more, and I thought about Dad and what he'd said, but I couldn't pull away. She held onto me, with our faces pressed together, and she kissed me on the ear a few times and I guess I did, too, I mean I kissed her on the ear, and now and then we kind of whispered things.

"Bobbie . . ."

"Yeah?"

"This is kind of like that day over at your house, isn't it?

When Daddy raised all that big fuss over nothing."

"We weren't doing anything," I said. "We weren't doing a darned thing."

"He's crazy," she said. "Anyway, well even if we had been, what difference would it've made? He does it, he and Mama. If it's so bad, why—"

"Josie," I said. "For gosh sake, are you crazy? You know good and well that's—well, it's not the same."

She said, all right, if that was the way I felt, if I was going to get mad every time she opened her mouth. So I said what the heck was wrong with her, who was getting mad, and I kissed her again to prove that I wasn't.

"Bobbie . . . did you ever?" she said.

"Huh-uh," I said.

"If I . . . promise you'll never tell anyone if I tell you something?"

"Well, sure," I said.

She hesitated. Then, she put her mouth real close to my ear and whispered.

"Aw," I said. "You're kidding."

"All right," she said. "I don't care if you don't believe me."

I swallowed. My mouth seemed kind of all full of spit all of a sudden. "W-Who—when, Josie?"

"Last summer. When I was going into town one Saturday. I was almost to the station and this man, I don't know who he was, but anyway he had a big car, and he asked me if I didn't want a ride. So . . ."

"Gosh," I said, "you hadn't ought to've gone with him, Josie. He—why, he might have been crazy or somethin' and—"

"Pooh." She shrugged. "People just make those stories up to scare their kids."

"The heck they do," I said. "You read about guys like that in the newspapers all the time. They get a girl in their car, and then they—after they've done it they get scared—and they, well, you've read about 'em yourself, Josie."

"Well," she shrugged again. "Well, anyway, I did. He did it to me."

I didn't say anything. I couldn't right then because I had to keep swallowing.

"He was sort of playing around," she said, "and after a while he drove off the highway and pulled up behind a big sign board. H-He"—she shivered and pulled me closer—"it hurt awful, Bobbie."

"Gosh," I said. "For gosh sake, Josie."

"I . . . I thought I was going to bleed all over everything. Even the second time when, well, you know, I shouldn't have . . ."

I swallowed again, hard, and she ran her hand through my hair. Then, she took her hand away and I could feel her fumbling for something down in her pants pocket. She, found it, finally, the thing she was looking for, and squeezed it into my hand.

"B-Bobbie. . . . You know what that is?"

"Yeah, I guess so," I said.

"I copped it out of Mama and Daddy's bedroom. I . . . are they all alike, Bobbie? I mean, will they fit anyone?"

"I guess so," I said. "Gosh, how do I know? I guess they will."

"Would they, you? W—Would that one?"

"I—Josie!" I said. "Josie, what—d-do you—"

"Wait," she said. "Wait a minute, Bobbie. Someone might see us here."

She pushed me away and stood up, and then she looked down at me kind of drowsy-like, her eyes narrowed, and held her hand out to me. I stood up, and we went back toward the cliff a little ways, where some bushes grew out of the base of it and there was a kind of little cave.

I got down on my knees and spread her sweater on the ground, and it was like a dream, me with that thing still clenched in my hand, and her getting down on the sweater and lying back. It didn't seem real at all and my head was pounding like sixty, and I was so choked up I could hardly breathe.

I sort of turned my back so she couldn't see when I put the thing on, and my hands kept fumbling and jumping, but finally I did it. I turned back around and there she was, just taking her time like it wasn't anything, unzipping the side of those goofy-looking shorts, and pulling the blouse up out of them, unbuttoning it and turning it back. And—

I was down on the ground with her, hugging and kissing and—

"Bobbie!" she said, kind of mad-laughing. "Now, wait a minute, silly!"

"J-Josie," I said. "F-For g-g-gosh—"

"You hear me, Bobbie? I'm going to be mad, now! Y-You'll—Please, Bobbie! W-Wait. We c-can't—you can't do it that . . . *Bobbie!*"

So we did it, and she didn't seem mad then, but afterwards she was. She said just to look at her and how could she go home with blood on her and it was all my fault and she had a good notion to tell her mother I'd made her.

"I'm sorry, Josie," I said. "For gosh sake, I didn't mean to. How many times I got to tell you that?"

"A lot of good that does," she said. "It's all your fault."

"Well, you'd better not blame it on me," I said. "You'd better not go blabbing to your folks about me."

"Ho, ho!" she said. "Well, I know I got to do something. You certainly can't expect me to take all the blame."

I began to get scared. I thought about Dad and the time Jack Eddleman had raised such a fuss, and, now, well, now, there was really something to fuss about, and if he acted that way then, what would he do now.

I could wash them out for you in the creek," I said. "You want me to do that, Josie?"

"Pooh!" She jerked away from me. "Cold water and no soap. A lot of good that would do!"

"Well," I said. "Well—uh—well, maybe—"

"Well, go on and say it," she said. "If you've got anything to say, say it!"

"I'm trying to, ain't I?" I said. "What do you think I'm trying to do, anyway? Shut up a minute, for gosh sake, and give me a chance."

"Well, go on," she said. "And don't you dare tell me to shut up, Mr. Bobbie Talbert!"

"Maybe—well, maybe," I said, "you could kind of sneak

up behind those bushes at the top of the cliff, and when you see your mother talking to someone you could slip around the block and come up the alley to your house and get into some other clothes."

"And what would I do with these?" she said. And then she said, "Well, I guess I could. I could spill ink on them or something and put them in the dirty clothes, and maybe, well, I guess that would be all right."

"Will you, Josie?" I said. "Will you do that?"

"Maybe."

"Promise," I said.

"Maybe. I will if I can."

"But why the heck can't you?" I said. "I told you just how to do it, and you said you could so what's the maybe about?"

She shrugged, looking at me out of the corner of her eyes. And I knew she would do it; she just had to and she knew it as well as I did, so why wouldn't she promise?

I guessed she must have been sore, and not entirely because of her clothes. She felt like I did now. I guessed, kind of sore and mean and tired and dirty-feeling. It was funny how you could feel one way a couple minutes before, and then just the opposite now. I felt just as crummy as she did, only I couldn't act like she did. I had to go on coaxing and begging her to promise.

"Look at me, Josie," I said. "I got some on my clothes, too, and I'm not mad. I don't try to make you feel bad about it."

"Oh, pooh," she said. "It's different with a boy. Anyway, it's all your fault. You don't have any right to be mad!"

"You wouldn't—you'll do it like I said, won't you, Josie?" I said. "Won't you, Josie?"

"I said I would. Maybe."

"No maybe, darn it! You've got to promise."

"Maybe. I said maybe, and I mean maybe," she said.

She gave me another of those looks out of the corner of her eyes. And I knew she was just being spitey; she just *had* to do it, doggone it. But, well, what if she didn't? A crazy old girl like that, there was no telling what she might do.

I began to get scareder. Scareder and sorer. All at once I grabbed her by the shoulders and shook her.

"I'll show you!" I said. "Doggone you, you promise or I'll—I'll—"

"Pooh, ho-ho," she said. "Just what will you do, anyway?"

"You'll see. You better promise," I said. "Promise?"

"Maybe," she said. "That's what I promise. Maybe, maybe, maybe, maybe, may—Bobbie! *D-Don't . . .*"

donald skysmith **6**

That was the morning after the *Star*'s quarterly report came out, and it had been a honey. Circulation up thirty thousand over the previous quarter, advertising up forty-three thousand lines. With a report like that under my belt, it was just about the last morning in the world I expected an ass-eating from the Captain. But he was already on the phone when I hit the office, and it wasn't to hand me a bouquet.

He kept on talking to the operator after I picked up the receiver and said hello.

"Now you're quite sure of that, miss," he was saying. "You're positive we still have a managing editor? Mr. Skysmith is still with us?"

"Yes, sir," she giggled. "H-He's—tee, hee—he's on the wire now, sir."

The stupid, silly bitch! Boy, maybe she thought that was an ass in her girdle, but she'd find out. It was pure mud from now on and I'd make her know it.

"You're positve," the Captain said. "It isn't someone posing as Mr. Skysmith? He has all the proper credentials?"

"No, sir. I mean, yes, sir. He's—hee, hee, hee . . ."

The goddamned rotten stinking little bitch! Laughing at me because I was getting the razz and thinking she could get away with it. Thinking, by God, I'd take it from every goddamned pissant in the plant just because I had to take it from that goddamned dried-up, bastardly, son-of-a-bitching old Fascist.

I made a fast shuffle through the clips on my desk, those from the opposition papers and those from ours. I couldn't see where we'd missed a thing. We had everything the opposition had, and we had it better and more of it.

"Well," the Captain said, "as long as you're positive, miss. Don, how are you this fine morning?"

How *was* I? How the hell would I be? "Fine, sir," I said, as the operator went off the wire. "How are you, Captain?"

"Wonderful," he said. "I tell you, Don, there's nothing like this mountain air. You'll have to come up some time."

"Thank you, sir," I said. "I'd like that very much." And I closed my eyes, thinking, *oh, you son-of-a-bitch, you don't know just how much I'd like to.*

I could picture myself up there in that castle, creeping into his room with its big twelve-by-twelve bed. It would be loaded down with teletype flimsies and probably if you dug deep enough you'd turn up every whore west of the Mississippi. But to hell with them. I'd burn them all up together. I'd say, "I got something hot for you, Captain," and then out with the good old gasoline and a handful of matches, and—

"Don," he said. "I've been very much worried about Teddy. How is she getting along?"

"Wha—" I squeezed my eyes open, and unclenched my teeth. "Why, all right, I hope, Captain. The doctors aren't very committal, but they believe the malignancy was confined to the left breast. It's largely a matter, now, of wait and see."

"Terrible." He clicked his tongue. "So young, so beautiful. A terrible, terrible thing."

You bastard! Oh, you son-of-a-bitch!

"Yes, sir," I said. "She's suffered a great deal."

"Terrible," he repeated. "I think those things are always so much harder when one has young children."

Whoremonger, filth-eater! Go on and turn the screws. Tickle that floozie. But one of these days, powie! A five-alarm fire . . .

"Well," he went on, "I suppose the situation could be worse. At least you have the satisfaction of knowing you're doing everything possible. The very best doctors and surgeons, the finest care without stint. That's something to be grateful for, isn't it, Don?"

"Yes, sir," I said. "Teddy and I are very grateful, Captain."

"A lovely girl, Don. Fine and uncomplaining and courageous. The children would be lost without her."

Monster, bastard, inhuman son-of-a-bitch. Keep it up! I'll reach right through the phone and grab you!

"Let's see, what are you making now, Don? Twenty-five thousand, isn't it?"

"Twenty-two fifty."

"Not enough," he said. "Oh, that's not nearly enough, Don. Why, if I had someone like Teddy to work for—someone who depended on me and whose very life depended on . . . Did you say something, Don?"

"N-No, sir," I said. "I—I just coughed, Captain."

"You should be making thirty-five thousand, Don. You're letting Teddy down. Oh, I know you *think* you're doing everything possible, but you can't know it. You simply haven't had the resources to try everything. If you were getting thirty-five thousand, now, twelve thousand five hundred more, it might make a big difference. It might mean life for Teddy and a mother for those little tots of yours and . . . Yes, Don? You said something?"

"No, sir," I said. "I didn't say anything, Captain."

He was silent for a moment. I eased my desk drawer open, got the cap off a pint of bourbon and took a big slug.

"Feel better?" he said. "Well, there's something I'd like you to do, Don. I want you to walk over to the window and stick your head out."

"Yes, sir," I said.

It was coming now. We were getting into the main stretch. I walked over to the window and stuck my head out. Oh, yes, yes, indeed. I did exactly as I was told. He'd know if I didn't, just as he'd known when I took that drink. The Captain always knew. Part of it was instinct, the bestial cunning you find in the very lowest of the animals, but he didn't depend entirely on that. Only a very small fraction of the people in the Captain's pay were employed on his newspapers. The rest were spies, *his* spies, and they knew every goddamned thing.

Once, years before, the Captain had told a managing editor to go out and get a cup of coffee. He was eating the poor bastard out, you see, telling him he was asleep at the switch. Well, the guy went down to a restaurant, but he wasn't a coffee drinker, it seems, so he took a glass of milk instead. And when he came back to the phone, the Captain fired him. He'd had a stool on his tail, and when the guy drank milk, whiz, the old axe.

The rotten, stinking, son-of-a-bi—

I picked up the telephone. "I'm back, Captain," I said.

"Good," he said. "Perhaps you can tell me whether it's raining or not?"

"No, sir," I said. "It's not raining."

"Very good," he said. "That checks with my information. You've taken a great load off my mind, Don. I was beginning to have some doubts as to whether you'd know if it was raining or not."

"Yes, sir," I said.

Goddammit, why couldn't he get on with it? I should have been talking to the news desk, the telegraph editor, the city editor; figuring out the play on the day's stories. I glanced at the clock, and Jesus! it was only twenty minutes until our early-noon went to bed. If it wasn't ready in twenty minutes there'd be overtime in composing, overtime in the press room, overtime in circulation— overtime! overtime! the lousy, filthy union bastards—and we'd hit the street late, and—

I'd kill him! By God, I *would* kill him! I'd sneak into that castle at night, and he'd be ass deep in teletype flimsies and whores, and I'd have that good old gasoline and those good old matches—big kitchen matches—and I'd burn him alive! *BURN HIM—*

"You had a story in your late-final yesterday, Don. A paltry eight lines back near the classified pages."

"Yes, sir? Yes, Captain?" He was crazy. If it was a good story we'd have played it.

"A rape-murder out in the Kenton Hills section. Some fourteen-year-old girl. Very badly handled, Don. Should have been right column front page or better still a center-page spread with banner and lots of art."

"B-But, Captain—" I took the receiver away from my ear and stared into the mouthpiece. He was crazy, by God. "But, sir, there's nothing—nothing at this stage, at any rate—to justify—"

"You don't think so, Don?"

"Well," I said, "of course, I could be wrong. But there doesn't seem to be anything. Our courthouse man talked to the district attorney, and he doesn't feel—"

"Perhaps you could change his mind, Don. Build a fire under him. Throw a few matches his way, if you get my meaning."

"Well, I—"

"What about this boy they're holding? This Talbert?"

"They're letting him go," I said, "for the present at least. He admits intimacy with the girl, but the rape if any would seem to have been the other way around. All the people in that neighborhood—her own parents, for that matter—say she was pretty much of a chaser. She'd take out after anything that wore pants while this boy, on the other hand, did everything he could to keep out of her—"

"But he was intimate with her."

"This one time, yes. But he was miles away at the time she was strangled. Honestly, Captain, I—"

"Can he prove that he was miles away?"

"Well—well, perhaps not. He doesn't have any ironclad alibi. But he went out to the golf course several days a week, we know that much. We know what kind of a boy he is—character-wise—and the kind of girl she was. Under the circumstances, the d.a. is reasonably satisfied that he's telling the truth. He went on to the golf course. She lingered in the canyon waiting for a chance to slip into her house and get her clothes changed. Someone came along and found her there—they've fixed the time of her death at about noon—and—"

"And who might that mysterious someone be, Don? Does the d.a. have another suspect?"

"Not at present, no," I said. "They think it might have been some hobo, someone that dropped off a freight there where they slow down for the trestle. I understand that quite a few tramps, because of the water and the trees—"

"But the d.a. doesn't have anyone in custody? Aside from Talbert, there are no other suspects and there is every chance that there will be no other?"

"Well—"

"We've flubbed a good story, Don. Moreover, we've been remiss in our duty to the public. We don't know the facts in this case. We haven't given the public the facts. Just what do we *know* about this boy, anyway? What do we *know* about his background, his character, what he might or might not do? How do we *know* the district attorney has done his job thoroughly? How do we *know* he isn't soft-headed or incompetent? We don't, do we? We don't have anything to go on but his word. We've failed our trust to our readers."

I shook my head. Hell, it was a juvenile case, wasn't it? How could you, with no real evidence to go on, smear a—

"It's a murder case, Don. Murder and rape. There's been too much hush-hush about these juvenile criminals. We've got to call a halt, and this is an ideal time to begin."

An ideal story, he meant. It had just about everything. Young love and sex and murder and mystery. With the opposition still playing ethical—

"We'll run them off the stands, Don. By the time they wake up, it'll be too late. It'll be *our* story with the readers."

"Yes, sir," I said. "But—"

But why not kidnap the kid and hang him from the flagpole? That would make a good story, too, and it wouldn't be any worse than this.

"Don't misunderstand me, Don. All we want is facts, no distortions or exaggerations. We find out everything we can about this boy. We see that the d.a. and the police do their jobs properly. That's all. We don't try the case in the newspaper."

Oh, we don't, huh? What the hell did he call it? All the

facts, all the dirt we could dig up and nothing to offset it. The "facts" and the d.a. doing his job—doing a job if he wanted to keep his.

"All right, sir," I said. "I understand."

"I read your quarterly report, Don. It's quite good."

"Thank you, sir," I said. "I thought you'd be pleased with it."

"Yes, it's good. For a man getting twenty-two thousand five hundred. My very best wishes to Teddy, Don, and please do everything you can for her."

He hung up.

I hung up.

I glanced at the clock, squeezed my forehead between my hands. It was too much, by God; a man can take just so goddamned much and then he's had it.

I snatched up the phone, called for a conference hookup and gave news, and telegraph and city desk the word on the late-noon. Then, I told the city editor, Mack Dudley, to drag his ass in, and, yes, those were the words I used.

He came in, carefully closing the door behind him. I waited until he started to sit down, and then I brought my fist down on my desk as hard as I could.

He jumped like he was shot out of a gun.

"What kind of crap is this?" I yelled. "What the hell kind of city editor are you? You get a prize story dumped in your lap, and just because I'm not around to write it for you, you louse it up! I'm through, get me? You think you can wander around in your goddamned sleep, and let me take the ass-eatings I'll—"

"Now, look," he said. "See here, Don—Mr. Skysmith. I don't—"

The phone rang.

"Excuse me, Mack," I said, picking it up. "Yes? Skysmith speaking."

"Don"—it was the Captain again—"I don't like to make any suggestions concerning your personnel, but . . ."

"Yes, sir?" I said. "I'm always delighted to have your suggestions on anything, Captain."

"That operator who handled my call a while ago; she

struck me as being a very intelligent young woman. I hope she isn't transferred to the night shift."

"No, sir," I said. "She won't be."

I'd put her on early swing. Drag her ass out of bed at three in the morning. That girdle full of mud she thought was an ass.

"I'd like her to stay on her present shift. Oh, yes, and you might give her a five-dollar raise . . . if, of course, that's agreeable with you."

"Yes, sir," I said. "I'll take care of it right away."

I wouldn't give her five inches if she was the last god-damned woman on earth. I'd cut her pay five bucks, and blame it on the business office. Say that I sent the raise through and they screwed it up.

"She may feel a little shy, Don, about expressing her appreciation. You tell her that I'll be very glad to get a note from her—that I'll be looking forward to it."

"Yes, sir," I said.

The lousy, filthy, bastardly, son-of-a—

william willis 7

It was obvious, as I stepped through the door, that Skysmith had gotten it from the Captain, and Dudley had gotten it from Skysmith. It was also obvious, since I had been summoned, that one William Willis was about to be handed a package.

Dudley gave me his very best glare, developed after long years of practice on freshman copy boys. Skysmith stared at me with a mixture of sadness and sternness.

That Skysmith slays me. Always making like a character out of *The Front Page*, always tossing his weight around and getting nothing but his ass out of joint. I never could figure out what the Captain saw in him. Not that he's a bad guy, you understand. Just a fathead who came up too fast.

I gave him, Skysmith, a pleasant good morning. I winked and grinned at Dudley. He harrumphed, getting slobber on his chin in the process. He brushed it away, quickly, adding another five-hundred watts to the glare.

"Putting you on a story," he barked. "Think you know how to handle one?"

"We-el, I don't know about that," I said. "A story, eh? Isn't that a little unusual to have a reporter do a story?"

"Now, goddam you," he said. "You keep on pulling that smart sarcastic crap and—"

"Just a moment," I held up my hand. "One moment, Mr. Dudley. I would like to quote you the Guild-*Star* contract as it pertains to the use of obscene and profane language by *Star* supervisory employees when addressing—"

"Stuff your goddamned contract!" He turned to Skysmith, pointing a trembling finger at me. "Don, you've got to do something about this character! He's destroying morale. I can't say anything—give an order to anyone— without him—"

He choked up, slobbering on his chin again, and I obligingly continued for him: he couldn't raise hell with someone just because he felt like raising hell. He couldn't fire anyone except for cause. He hadn't been able to since I'd organized the *Star* chapter of the Guild and become its shop steward.

"All right, Bill," Skysmith said. "We're all familiar with the contract provisions, so let's just drop the subject, huh? And, Mack, you lay off of Bill, too. Goddammit"— he scrubbed his forehead—"this is a newspaper, not a kindergarten. Honest to Christ, I don't know what the hell's wrong with some of you birds! All you can think about is sniping at each other, getting even, carrying on some goddamned stupid feud! It's got to stop, get me? By God, I—I'm—"

"I'm sorry," I said. And, right at the moment, I was sorry—for him. The way he looked, I couldn't help it. "What's the story, Don?"

"Sure," Mack said gruffly. "Bill and I don't mean any-thing; just kidding around."

"Well, all right," said Skysmith. "It's that rape-murder

out in Kenton Hills, the one that broke late yesterday. You
may have seen the second-section squib we carried on it?"

I shook my head. "I don't recall . . . Wait a minute," I
said. "You mean that juvenile case? The one where—"

"I mean a *murder* case," Skysmith said firmly. "Rape and
murder."

"Well," I said, "maybe I'm dumb—now, now, Mack!—
maybe I'm dumb, but where's the story? The girl was fourteen, the boy fifteen. We can't print a lot of dirt about—"

"Facts," said Skysmith. "Facts are what we can print."

I looked at him, and I think my eyebrows must have gone
up a couple of inches. "What are we going to hang those
facts on?" I said. "What's our justification for tossing our
last shred of ethics out the window? I could see it, when
and if they pick up the nut who knocked the girl off, but
just to go to town on a couple of kids who had a little . . ."

My voice trailed off. After a minute, I said, "Oh, *no!*
You're kidding. You're not going to imply the boy
killed . . ."

"What the hell's wrong with it?" Skysmith wouldn't look
at me. "The kid got in, didn't he? He was there at the scene
of the crime, wasn't he? He can't prove, positively, that he
wasn't there at the time she was killed. He went on to the
golf course—he says—but he didn't go all the way. He was
about a quarter of a mile away when he saw that there were
only a few players out and a hell of a gang of caddies, so—"

"I know all that," I said. "The guys were kicking it around
over at the Press Club. The d.a. knows it, too, and he
doesn't feel there's sufficient grounds for charging the kid."

"Goddammit"—Skysmith brought his hand down on his
desk. "I didn't say the kid was guilty. But how the hell we
going to know unless we get all the facts? We don't know a
goddamned thing about him, Bill. What his background is,
what his reputation for—uh—truth and veracity is, what
the folks out in that neighborhood, his playmates and
teachers and so on think of him. All we've got to go on is
hearsay, just what that lardassed d.a. says, and you know
that stupid son-of-a-bitch, Bill. I'll bet he still hangs up his
socks on Christmas Eve."

"I don't know," I said. "I've always thought he was a pretty good man. As public officials go, of course."

"I'll tell you what I think," said Mack Dudley. "We give this the full treatment—get the facts like Don says and pour the coal on the d.a., I'll bet the kid cracks. I'll bet he confesses he took it away from that poor girl and then killed her to keep her from telling."

"Oh, I agree absolutely," I said. "I'm confident of it, Mack. In fact, I'd go a step further than that. I'll wager that if the *Star* gave you the treatment and sicced the d.a. on you, you'd confess to the crime yourself. Incidentally, and nothing personal intended, but where were you around noon yesterday?"

"Now, Bill," said Skysmith. "For Christ's sake—"

"You refusing to handle the story?" Mack snarled. "Go on! Tell me you won't do it!"

"Isn't there some alternative?" I said. "Something clean like scrubbing out the john? I haven't had much experience, but I'm strong and willing to learn."

"He refuses," said Mack. "According to paragraph six, clause b, the refusal of an editorial employee to—"

"Shut up!" Skysmith yelled. "Goddammit, SHUT UP! . . . Now, look, Bill, this is a perfectly legitimate story. It violates orthodox newspaper practice, perhaps, but there's nothing—uh—essentially wrong with it. All we want is the facts, no distortions or exaggerations. All we ask of the district attorney is a thorough investigation. That's not unreasonable, is it? There's nothing wrong with that?"

I shrugged. "Nothing I know of," I said, "that you don't."

He scrubbed his forehead again, his eyes squeezed shut. He opened them and leaned forward. "That's the way it stands," he said, and his voice was steady but there was an undercurrent of trembling in it. "You're a good reporter, and I'd like to see you handle the story. But it's going to be done, regardless. We've got other good reporters, and they aren't trouble makers. They're too busy with their jobs to fool around with unions. Now, what do you want to do?"

"Take you before the NLRB," I said, "on charges of penalizing an employee for union activity. But I suppose you'd call me a liar."

"That's right," he nodded evenly. "I'm giving you this assignment solely because you're the best man for the job. I mean that, Bill. You're a good reporter and I'd hate to lose you. Your union activities don't figure in the matter in any way."

I nodded absently, lighting a cigarette to gain time. Someone would do it, if I didn't. There was no question about that. The Captain had hollered frog, so jumping was the order of the day. And dammit, it would make a hell of a good story. Yes, sir, a hell of a story! Young love and sex and murder and mystery, and Christ, the color, the human interest! That Captain. You had to hand it to the decadent old buzzard. He didn't have any more principles than those maggots in his brain, but he knew story. He knew what would sell papers.

"Well, Bill?"

"It would make a good story," I said. "But practically anything will if you don't give a damn about decency and—"

"Save it. Yes or no?"

Well. It was going to have to be yes, naturally; a no would get me nothing but my time—without severance pay. Still, I hated to say yes, if for no other reason than that they felt I had to say it. If there's anything I like less than being pushed around it's being pushed around. A thing like this—taking a shove from old Fuddy Dudley and Donald the Great—could be very bad for my reputation.

Now, surely, I thought, *there should be something; you have to take it, but there must be some way of handing it back. No? Yes? Think fast, Mr. Willis.*

So I thought very fast, and a very beautiful idea came to me. I heaved an enormous sigh of surrender—more apparent than real—and said that I would gladly accept the assignment.

"I suppose this is exclusively my story," I said. "There won't be three or four other guys backtracking or anticipating me?"

"Oh, it's your story all right," Mack Dudley grinned. "No one's but yours. We'll have his byline on every page, won't we, Don?"

Skysmith gave him a frown, and nodded to me. "It's all yours, Bill. Of course, we'll be getting some side and feature stuff from the trained seals—you get 'em to work on that, Mack—but the running story will be yours."

"That's fine," I said.

"Incidentally, watch yourself if you run into any of the opposition boys. If they knew what we were up to they'd jump in ahead of us. We'll get this thing all set today, get it all lined up, and tomorrow we'll hit 'em with it. They'll never know what happened until it's too late."

"Swell. What about the d.a.?" I said. "Do I goose him today?"

"Yes—no." Skysmith hesitated. "No, we'll let the story be the goose. Let him sleep, see, so we can point it out. Here's a public official who's so damned lazy and stupid that the *Star* has to do his job for him. We burn his ass so hard he's jumping sideways to put out the fire."

"I get you," I said. "Now, there's one thing I'm a little worried about, Don. I don't know whether you've thought about it or not, but . . ."

"Yes, Bill?" He smiled at me, relaxed, the conqueror magnanimous to the conquered.

"Do you suppose there's any danger that this thing will backfire on us? It's pretty rough, you know, a big paper landing on a fifteen-year-old kid with all four feet. The public might not like it."

"Well"—he frowned faintly—"well," he shrugged, "of course, we'll have to use some judgment. We can't go too far overboard. But leave that part to me. You just get the story, everything you think we ought to have, and I'll check it over myself; tone it down if I feel it needs it."

The hell you will, Donald. It's MY story. I said, "Well, that does it, I guess. Now, I don't phone, anything in, right? I get the facts, and then I come in and write the story."

"Right. Try not to be too late, but take as much time as you have to. Mack and I will be waiting."

I nodded, and got up from my chair. He stood up, too, and stuck out his hand. As I've said, he wasn't a bad guy, even if he was a fathead. But he had pushed me around, and I do not like to be pushed.

"Good boy," he said. "You do us the right kind of job on this, Bill, and maybe I can swing a bonus."

"Oh, I'm glad to do it," I said. "I don't expect any bonus, Don."

I got some copy paper from my desk, and picked up a photographer. We drove to the courthouse, and I had a private chat with the district attorney. I told him about the little surprise the *Star* had planned for him.

He was pretty damned sore about it, and, needless to say alarmed. He was also very grateful to me for tipping him off.

william willis 8

They didn't have the boy, Robert Talbert, in the jug proper. There were a couple of witness rooms with a connecting door adjoining the district attorney's office, and he was in one and a jail matron in the other.

The d.a. told the matron to catch some air, about an hour's worth. Then, after introducing me and the photog to the boy, he went back to his office and left us alone.

The kid was about on a par with a good many teenagers I've seen. They aren't watchful exactly. They aren't exactly sullen. There is rather a look of resigned hopefulness about them: they look as though no good can possibly come to them, albeit they would certainly welcome a little and are rightfully entitled to it.

I do not recall that kids looked that way in my day. I think it must be the times, this age we live in, when the reasons for existence are lost in the struggle to exist.

He looked from me to the photographer, cautiously,

trying to smile—but not too much. The kind of smile that can change quickly into a frown.

"I t-thought I was going home," he said. "They told me I was going home."

"You are," I said. "You'll get there all right, Bob. You don't mind talking to me a little first, do you? You don't have to, understand, but I'll sure catch hell from my editor if you don't."

"Well . . ." He scuffed his foot against the floor. "What you want to talk about? I already told everything there was to tell."

"But you haven't told me," I pointed out. "Now, let's get busy—cigarette?—or they'll have you out of here before I can get my story."

He took a cigarette, and we sat down. He started talking, moving right along with it without being prodded. I took him backwards and forwards through it. I took him from the middle back and from the end to the middle. He didn't trip up. It came out the same way each time.

He got his foot wet as he started to cross the canyon creek. While he was drying out, the girl showed up. They played around a while and then they had it. She got blood on her clothes and blamed him for it. He tried to get her to promise she wouldn't tell her mother. She was sore, wanting to make him sweat, so she stalled. He got sore and shook her. She promised, and he went on toward the . . .

"Hold it a minute, Bob," I said. "Show me how you shook her. Maybe you'd better stand up."

He stood up and thrust his hands out, curving them as though he was gripping something. I gave the photographer the nod. He crouched down in front of the kid, and shot up at him.

A shot like that, as you may know, distorts the features, gives them a grim macabre look. With that cigarette tucked in the corner of his mouth and his hands clawing the air, the kid would look like Horrible Bill from Killerdill.

We got a few other nice poses from him while he was still on his feet, and then I had him sit down and went back to the story.

"Now, let's see if I've got this straight, Bob. You cut across country to the golf links, up the other side of the canyon and through the woods and on through the fields and another patch of woods, and so on. About four miles, and you didn't see anyone in all that distance? Either coming or going."

"Huh-uh. I don't think I saw anyone. I might have, but not to notice."

"Then you came to this knoll overlooking the golf links, about a quarter of a mile away, and you decided it wasn't worthwhile going down. So you just sat down there, by yourself with nothing to do, and you stayed there for more than three hours. Why, Bob? Why didn't you go on home?"

"I told you." He frowned impatiently. "I told you about six times already. I couldn't go home. I was supposed to be in school, and I couldn't go home until it was time for it to be out."

"Sure, you couldn't. Of course not," I said. "And no one could see you there, either, could they? There's no road nearby, no houses."

"I don't know if anyone saw me or not," he said. "What I said was I didn't see anyone."

"I see," I nodded. "You'll have to excuse me for having such a lousy memory, Bob. I don't like to keep bothering you, but if I don't get this story right I might get fired."

"Well," he said grudgingly, "that's all right."

"Now, this girl, Josie. I suppose you know she'd had intercourse several times. It was only once with you, wasn't it? Just the one—"

"Yes! How many times I got to tell you?"

"Did you want to do it again? Did you ask her?"

"I didn't want to do it the first time! Well, I did afterwards you know, after she started to—to—"

"What do you suppose she'd have done if you'd tried to do it again? Would she have been sore?"

"Maybe. How do I know? What's the difference?" he said, and he brushed at his eyes. "I—I d-don't want to talk about her. How would you feel if someone you'd known all your life, s-someone you saw every day—and—and maybe you thought they were kinda crazy and always hanging around when you didn't want 'em b-but—"

He choked and turned his head. "She was p-pretty nice," he said. "M-Me and Josie, well, we always liked each other."

"Naturally," I said. "Of course, you did. Now, Bob, what about . . ."

I took him through the story again. It came out a carbon copy of the earlier tellings. And was that as it should be? Or wasn't it just a little bit odd?

Shouldn't it, if it was the truth, vary a little from time to time?

It was like a recitation, something he'd memorized.

"Just a few more questions, Bob . . . As long as you were so near the golf course, why didn't you go on? After all—"

"I been tellin' and tellin' you, mister! Because it wouldn't have been any use! I could see the parking lot from up there and the caddie shack, and I knew I wouldn't get no— any job."

"You couldn't be positive, Bob. You couldn't have lost anything by it. You could have got yourself a cold drink, kidded around with the boys, while you were waiting until time to go home."

He licked his lips, hesitantly. He talked very straightfor-wardly upon the main story line, what had transpired between him and the girl and so on, but these tangential angles—things of nominally minor importance—seemed to disturb him.

"I told you," he said. "I didn't want a drink. I didn't want to kid around."

"And you had some blood on your trousers? You thought someone might ask about it?"

"Yes! It was partly that, maybe. I guess it was."

"You must have noticed the blood before you ever started to the—"

"I did notice it! I told you I did."

"Well, as long as you didn't want anyone to see you why go all the way out to—?"

"I had to go some place, didn't I? An' I didn't say I didn't want anyone to see me! I—well, I didn't maybe. I guess I didn't. But if there'd been any point to it, if I could've got a job or anything, I would—"

"Uh-huh. I understand. Now, you were about a quarter of a mile away from the course. You could look down and see the caddies and the players. Isn't that right?"

"I could see 'em, but not to recognize. I could just see how things looked—that there wasn't any use going on."

"Then, they—someone probably saw you, too, huh? Not to recognize, but—"

"No, they couldn't! I told you that. I could see them, but they couldn't see me."

"You were trying not to be seen?"

"Yes!"

"But, why, Bob?"

"I told you, mister, for gosh sake! I s-seen—I wasn't going to unless there was some sense to it, was I, an' when I seen—s-saw there wasn't any, I couldn't get a job, w-why I didn't. For gosh sake, I keep explainin'—"

"Sure. I understand," I said.

And I did. It wasn't logical but it was believable, reasonable, if you put yourself in his place. He was explaining the inexplicable, a matter of feeling rather than thinking, and insofar as it could be done he was doing a pretty fair job of it. Once when I was a kid, I mixed salt in the sugar bowl, and at dinner that night—and I was the only member of the family who took sugar in tea—I spooned a gob of it into my cup. Dopey? Sure, it was, when I look back on it now. But at the time I did it it seemed perfectly right and proper. I couldn't have told you why I did it, but I didn't see how I could have done anything else.

Of course, that wasn't the same as this. I wasn't the same as this kid. He had his story down too pat. He was too straightforward in one way—upon certain points—and not enough in another. After all, as long as he was practically there at the golf links, as long and *if*—

"Can I go home now, mister? You said I could."

"Sure." I jerked my head at the photographer and got up. "I'll speak to the district attorney, Bob."

No, it wasn't the same, all right. This was different. I was rationalizing, hoping subconsciously that the kid was guilty. I couldn't be impartial. I was using him, swinging him as the club in my grudge play against the *Star*; I was going to knock his brains out in the course of trepanning Dudley and Skysmith, and I needed justification. If he was guilty, good. If he was innocent, bad. Very bad. That would make me a supersonic jet-propelled heel instead of the slow-flying, propeller-driven model which I had become reasonably well adjusted to.

I had another talk with the d.a. before I left. I told him I couldn't make up my mind about Talbert. He seemed to be leveling but, well, I just didn't know. I'd rather not say anything. After all, he was just a kid and even if he was guilty he probably hadn't realized what he was doing. He'd just got scared, and . . .

"Well"—the d.a. searched my face—"I'm by no means satisfied with his story, Bill. I slept on it last night, and I'd already made up my mind before you came in this morning that he had a great deal to explain. It was my own decision, understand. I've never allowed myself to be coerced, and I'm certainly not going to begin now. I'm not going to railroad some youngster just to make a Roman holiday for—"

"Of course, not," I said. "I understand, Clint. All you want is to get at the truth."

"Ab-solutely!"

"Take it easy on him, will you, Clint? I know *you* will, but some of these county dicks—I imagine you'll want to, uh, divide the responsibility, have some assistance in the questioning—"

"You don't need to ask that, Bill. If there's one thing I do not and have never tolerated, it's abuse of a prisoner."

"Swell," I said. "I'll just run along then, and . . . and you'll get in touch with me? When and if."

"You can depend on it." He shook my hand earnestly. "You did me a very great favor, and I never forget a favor."

. . . The kid's teacher, a Miss Brundage, was a pretty tough nut to crack. One of those "fair" people. You could boot her in the tail, and she'd probably say you were giving her a spinal adjustment.

Yes, Robert had been truant a lot, but no more so or even as much, as a great many other boys. Yes, he did get a little out of hand at times, but he was at the restless age. Most boys went through a stage of unruliness; she'd seen very few who didn't. And she didn't believe Robert felt very well. She felt that there might be a situation at home that, uh—

"Yes?" I said.

But, no. She'd only talked with Mrs. Talbert one time, and she'd never met Mr. Talbert. She didn't know them well enough to have formed an opinion. All she knew was that they were long-time residents of the community, and everyone spoke very highly of them. They were really, she was sure, very nice well-adjusted people, just as Robert was really a very nice well-adjusted boy.

She'd come out in the corridor to talk to me, and she kept having to stick her head back in the classroom and call for order. She didn't get it; there were just too dammed many kids jammed in too small a space. The moment she turned her back the racket started up again. Cat-calls and flying chalk and grab-assing.

I kept on talking to her. The kids kept bellowing. Her smile began to tighten up, and a glint came into her eyes. There was a rising tremoloish note to her voice, like you hear from an offtune key of c fiddle string. A tiny vein throbbed in her throat, and she almost yanked the door off its hinges when she had to speak to the kids.

I could see she was cracking up. She was just about to explode. She was irritated with me, and annoyed with the kids. She had to cut loose on someone and you know who that someone was.

The explosion came. She clouded up and rained all over one Robert Talbert who, it suddenly appeared, was just about the most wilful, sullen, uncooperative, hateful youth she'd ever come up against. "Honestly, Mr. Willis! I do want to be fair, and I'm sure he isn't entirely to blame, but . . ."

She was still raving when the photographer and I left her.

I was going to stop by the principal's office, but I remembered suddenly that he'd somehow got himself on the *Star*'s heel list. Some speech he'd made at a teachers' convention one time had rubbed the Captain the wrong way. No paper in the *Star* chain would have quoted him or printed his name if he'd sailed the Atlantic in a salad bowl, so I passed him by.

There was a lunch room and soda fountain across the street from the school. The guy who ran it was a cranky old bastard who was convinced that the younger generation was hell-bound on a handcar. No respect for their elders. Always sneaking candy bars and chewing gum, slipping out without paying their checks. Buying a nickel coke and loafing around, slopping it all over everything, until they'd read every magazine in the place. None of 'em were any good. Not a danged one.

He wouldn't say that that Talbert kid was any worse than the rest. At least, he wouldn't say it at first. But he got around to it. Yes, sir, that Talbert was a real bad one, the ringleader of the crowd. Should have locked him up long ago. . . .

The photographer and I went over to the Talbert neighborhood. I went from door to door, and while I didn't hit pay dirt at every house I still got plenty. The kid had lived there all his life, fifteen whole years. Any kid will pull some out-of-the-way stunts in that time, or if he doesn't he might as well. He'll still be accused of them.

So . . .

So there were windows that had been broken and trash barrels set on fire and ugly words chalked on sidewalks. There were little girls who'd been chased ("and we hadn't done *anything*") and a woman who'd seen someone peeking in her bathroom window ("and I'm almost positive now that I think about it . . .") and an old maid who'd been followed home from the station one night, and she *was* positive period.

There was a lot more evidence in the case of *Friends and Neighbors* vs. Robert Talbert, but I see no need to set it down here. It was about par for the course, about what you might dig up on me if you visited around my childhood neighborhood—and *if* I was in jail on suspicion of murder at the time of your inquiry.

It's amazing, you know, honestly amazing, that any crime is ever committed. Because I've never yet talked to the associates or acquaintances of a miscreant who didn't know all along that he was a thoroughly bad egg. He didn't *act* right, you know. He couldn't look you straight in the eye (or he looked too straight). He talked too much (or he didn't talk enough). Oh, they knew he was a crook all right, knew he was about to pull a fast one. So why didn't they stop him, why didn't they mention their suspicions? Well . . .

You tell me.

Talbert hadn't gone to work, naturally, and he and the missus were both home. They'd been expecting the boy's release all day, and she blew her top at the news that he was being held indefinitely. I'd been sure she would; you could see the sub-surface hysteria in her eyes, hear it in the high-pitched, too-rapid speech. She'd probably always been a little flighty, and the menopause hits that kind hard.

Mr. Talbert tried to comfort her—he looked like he could stand some comforting himself—and she turned on him. It was his fault! He'd driven Bobbie to it! Always nagging and scolding and picking on the boy. Treating him like a man when he was only a baby.

"You drove him to it! Yes, you did! Y-You . . . !"

Talbert took it as long as he could. Then, he began to unwind. She hadn't made a home for the boy. She was always chasing around, gossiping with the neighbors, instead of taking care of the house. She hadn't acted like a mother should. She'd embarrassed and shamed the kid so much with her doggone nuttiness that he was afraid to bring any friends to the house. He'd had to meet them outside, and they were the wrong kind, naturally, and—

The photographer started shooting them. They clammed up fast, shamed and scared, realizing, I guess, that in taking out their peeves on each other they'd as good as admitted the boy's guilt.

Talbert told us to get out. He seemed to mean it, so we did.

We went a few doors down the street to the Eddlemans', the parents of the dead girl.

They'd been assuaging their sorrow with a bottle, and they'd had enough to be pretty talkative. Oddly enough, or at least it seemed odd to me, they were reluctant to knock the kid. They didn't see how Bobbie could have done a thing like that. Of course, if he *had* done it, he ought to be—

"But I'd hate to think he did," Eddleman said. "It's kind of hard to believe that he did. I never cared much for the kid, y'understand, one of these close-mouthed kind that acted like it'd bust his ribs if he laughed. But . . ."

"I know what you mean," I said. "I suppose he'd just about have to be like that, don't you? I don't know much about his parents, but I imagine they could get a kid down in time."

His eyes flashed, and his big red face turned a shade or two redder. "You got something there, mister," he grunted. "That old man of his, old frozen-face, there ain't a soul I know that'll say a good word for him. He's just plain damned mean, get me? And quick tempered! Why, just the other day, now, I tried to pass a little joke with him—remember, Fay, I told you about it—and I actually thought he was going to murder me!"

"That's right, Mr. Willis," Fay Eddleman nodded vigorously. "That's exactly the way he is. And his mother! An absolute lunatic, if there ever was one. You can be going along, minding your own business, and here she'll come, and—and she'll just act awful! Just say the dirtiest, craziest things she can think of!"

"Oh, she's nuts all right," Eddleman said. "Crazy as a bedbug. But she can't hold a candle to the old man. A regular maniac, and he's a crook, too. I sold a house to a party one time that'd done some business with him, and he said . . ."

We talked a while longer; they did, rather. And you probably know the conclusion they reached.

He'd done it all right, they decided. He'd tried to assault

the girl once before, and there'd been plenty of other indications that he was a murderer in the making. They'd seen it coming on for a long time. He was guilty as hell, the dirty little skunk, but his parents were guiltier. They were *really* responsible and they ought to be punished right along with him.

. . . The photographer and I took a quick whirl through the shopping center. That wrapped it up. I told the photog to pull me three extra prints on each of the pictures. Then, I let him go and went home to my apartment.

I wrote the story there, or, rather, it almost wrote itself, making an original and three copies. I sorted the various pages out, and read back through it.

It was something, believe me. There hadn't been any thing like it since the *Graphic* folded. I thought of what Skysmith was going to say, and I laughed out loud. I read back through the thing again.

That kid . . . Jesus, this was going to be pretty bad for him! But—well, I hadn't invented anything, had I? I hadn't exaggerated? No (I answered myself), I hadn't.

The dirt was there, and I'd dug for it. Dug pretty hard. But I hadn't put a gun to anyone's head. I'd simply talked and let them talk, spilling out the dirt that was in them.

I poured myself a drink. I gulped it down and had a few more. I went back through the story again. And this time the doubts, the hunch, I'd had that morning began to grow. These people thought the kid was guilty. The people who knew him best, his own parents, thought he was guilty. There wasn't any real evidence, when you tried to pin it down. It was the sort of stuff you might dig up on almost any kid. Still—well, what if it was? It wasn't anything to his credit, was it? It certainly didn't prove he was innocent, did it?

And so many people felt the same way about him. And he'd acted pretty damned shifty when I'd talked to him. He had this story down too pat. He was too straightforward . . . and not straightforward enough. He hadn't seemed very sorry about the girl, just sort of dull and defiant. And . . .

Well, he could be guilty as easily as not. I wouldn't say

that he was, but I wouldn't say that he was innocent, either.

I fixed myself a bite to eat, and had a few more drinks. The phone rang repeatedly and I let it. It would be the office, Dudley or Skysmith, wondering what the hell had happened to me. I wasn't ready to go in yet, for several reasons.

A messenger arrived with the extra prints of the pictures. I sorted them into stacks and put them with the dupes on the stories.

The phone rang three times and stopped. I picked it up and dialed the d.a. He said the kid was cracking. He'd sent the detectives out to dinner, and they'd work on him some more afterwards.

"I imagine we'll have to bury him," he said, "I'm surprised we haven't been hit with a writ before this."

"So am I," I said. "Where are you taking him, Clint?"

"Well . . . You really want to know, Bill?"

"No," I said. "I guess I don't. I don't know anything. Just call me at the office when you have the news."

. . . It was about ten o'clock when I went in, a little more than an hour before the presses started to roll on the early-morning edition. Only a few dog-trick men were scattered around the big city room. Dudley had given up and gone home, but Don Skysmith was still in his office. He jumped up, scowling, when I walked in.

"Jesus, God, Bill, what the hell kept you? Is that the story? Well, give it to me, for Christ's sake!"

He yanked the pages out of my hand. I sat down across the desk from him, and pulled the early-morning dummy in front of me.

He grunted, startled. He let out a howl and slapped the desk with his hand. "For God's sake, Bill! What the hell is this?"

"Yes?" I said. "Is there something wrong, Mr. Skysmith?"

"Something wrong! Why, goddammit"—he thrust the story at me—"are you out of your goddamned mind? Get out of here! Get out there to a typewriter, and do this like it should be done. You know damned well we can't—"

"Mr. Skysmith," I said, "that story will run exactly as it is written. Exactly, understand? In fact, I'm going to see it through the composing room and onto the presses."

"*Huh?*" He stared at me, open mouthed. "Are you—"

"Yes," I said, "it will run as written, Mr. Skysmith, or it will not run at all." *Push me around, will you, you phony?*

He said I was crazy, again, I was out of my goddamned mind. He scrubbed at his forehead. "Look, Bill. I—I—" His lips trembled in his taut, pale face. "I know how hard you must have worked on this. I k-know how it is when you're a reporter and you knock yourself out on something and t-then some desk man tells you it—it— Just let it go, Bill, and I'll take care of it. My wife's pretty sick and I was in kind of a hurry to—"

"Donald," I said. "Your majesty. The story runs as is."

"It can't! It— What the hell you mean, calling me—?"

"You wanted dirt," I said. "You got it."

"Goddamn you, I didn't want anything like this! I told you we had to use some judgment, we had to be careful! This is—is—it's outrageous! We'll get a bad reaction from it. We're pulling the switch on the kid. Why, goddammit, the Captain would blow his top if—"

"Suppose we leave it to the Captain?" I said.

"*What?* You know we—"

"Call him up," I said. "Tell him you tried to push the wrong guy around, and he's got you over a barrel. Tell him . . ."

I told him what to tell the Captain. The story would go into the *Star* as it was written. Otherwise, I'd give it to the three opposition papers. They'd print it if they thought we were going to. In any event, and if they did tone it down, our scoop would be shot. The Captain was looking forward to this surprise party. He meant to run the other sheets off the stands. Now there wouldn't be any surprise, and the *Star* would probably do a little running itself.

"Oh, yes," I said, "you might also tell him I've got the confession on ice. Ask him if he'd like to see it in the *Star* after it comes out in the opposition."

His mouth moved wordlessly. Slowly, he sank down into his chair.

"Y-You—you won't get away with this, Willis! I'll get you and that lousy d.a. if—"

"You mean you're going to admit you're a sap?" I said. "I don't think you will, Donald. The Captain might forgive a bit of faulty judgment—over-enthusiasm—but he doesn't have much use for chumps. It's almost a phobia with him, you know. He hates 'em like crazy. Now, sons-of-bitches, he doesn't mind. He—"

"Like you, huh? Like you for example."

"Oh, well," I said. "I wasn't asking for compliments. . . . May I?"

I pulled the story and art across the desk. I took a pencil out of my pocket.

He said, "Bill . . . why, Bill? What's it all about?"

"You pushed me around," I said. "I do not like to be pushed around." Especially by a man who never *was* a real newspaperman.

"But—but I didn't! I haven't! I've never meant to, anyway. God, you don't hold Dudley against me, do you? I have to back up my city editor."

I didn't answer him. I bent over the papers.

His desk drawer opened; there was the scrape of metal against glass and the smell of whiskey.

He said, "What are you doing, Bill?" And I looked up.

"I'm writing heads," I said, evenly. "I'm captioning pictures. I'm fixing up the dummy. Pretty handy, huh? No need to bother with copy men or picture desk or news editor. I can get the stuff and I can write the stuff, and then I can carry it right on through the mill and I can do it better than any son-of-a-bitch in the shop. I could even set it up on the lino, if I had a card, and I could lay it out on the stone. I don't need to take anyone's word for what's right. I can tell them. Because I'm a newspaper man, get me? An all around, two-handed man. It's all I've ever done, all I ever want to do. Take me away from newspapers and I'd die, and I'd want to die. And you can't understand that, can you, Skysmith? You can't because you're not a newspaper man. You're just a punk who got the breaks. A college boy who lucked himself into a Pulitzer and rode it for all it was worth. You're . . . well, skip it."

He took another drink, hesitated, and pushed the bottle across the desk. I pretended not to see it.

"I see, Bill," he said, quietly. "I'm beginning to understand why . . ."

I shrugged. I felt uncomfortably empty, drained dry. "Don't jump to conclusions, Don. I was just popping off."

"I understand," he said. "I know how you must feel about me."

"Why, Don"—I forced a grin and stood up—"I had no idea you cared. As a matter of fact, I love you like a brother. Come along, huh? Come with me to the composing room."

"I guess not," he said. "You don't need me, Bill."

"Sure, I do," I said. "What the hell? Two heads are better than one any old day."

"I'd better go home," he said. "My wife . . . my wife is pretty sick."

richard yeoman 9

The d.a. locked the door on the kid, and handed me a five. Two fifty for me and two fifty for Charlie Alt. He said we should get our supper, and not to take all night about it.

"And no gabbing, understand?" he said. "You don't know a thing about the Talbert boy."

"What about him?" I said. "You want we should bring him a sandwich or something?"

"No," he said. "When he's ready to eat, he can say so."

"We could bring him a malt or something," I said. "Something cold to drink maybe."

"He can have something to drink," he said, "whenever he wants it."

"Well, I was just asking," I said.

"He can have anything he wants," the d.a. said. "Just as soon as he comes to his senses."

Me and Charlie figured the Chinaman's was the best deal, being close and pretty reasonable and all, so we went downstairs and headed across the street. Charlie was kind of mumbling to himself and counting on his fingers. Finally, he got it figured out.

"Small steak, french fries, peas, pie, two cups of coffee," he said. "Two fifty exactly, Dick."

"Yeah," I said, "but what about the tip?"

"H---," he said, "what you want to tip Chinamen for? They got a lot more money than you have."

"Oh, I don't know," I said. "I guess maybe I shouldn't, but I always feel kind of funny. Don't you tip 'em, Charlie?"

"Well, I ain't·going to tonight," he said.

We got to the Chinaman's and I told Charlie to go on back and get us a booth. I had to give my old lady a ring.

"I guess I ought to call my daughter, too," he said, giving me a kind of funny look. "You go ahead and I'll wait for you."

"No, you better go get us a booth," I said. "You hold it until I'm through, and then I'll hold it while you're talking."

Well, H---," he said. "There's plenty of d----d booths." But he went on back.

I called Kossy at his office but I didn't get any answer, and he wasn't to home either. Finally, I got him over at U.S. Federal where they was having a night immigration hearing.

"Dick Yeoman, Mr. Kossmeyer," I said. "Mr. Kossmeyer, ain't you counsel in the Talbert case?"

"Talbert?" he said. "Tal—oh, yeah. Sure, Dick. They let the kid go."

"No, they ain't let him go," I said. "It don't look like they're going to either, if you know what I mean. I was going to call you earlier, Mr. Kossmeyer, but I didn't have a chance and—"

"S-- of a b---h!" he said. "I supposed he was home in bed. I haven't had a peep out of his folks."

"I've been doing everything I can for that boy, Mr. Kossmeyer," I said. "But frankly that ain't very much. It ain't something I got a lot of control over, if you follow my meaning."

"Sure," he said, quickly. "I appreciate that, Dick. You— stop by my office tomorrow. Where—"

"Oh, that's not necessary," I said. "What time, Mr. Kossmeyer?"

"Any time, any time!" he said. "Where've you got him, Dick?"

"At county, Mr. Clinton's office," I said. "But I kind of got a hunch we're moving him."

"J---s!" he said. "You know what the angle is, Dick, why— Never mind. Where are you burying him, any idea?"

"I honestly don't know, Mr. Kossmeyer," I said. "The d.a. ain't saying very much, if you know what I—"

"Son of a b---h!" he said. "Those G-d D----d dimwitted Talberts! I ought to sue 'em for mopery!"

"Some people is certainly stupid all right," I said. "But I guess in a kind of crisis like this they're probably kind of out of their minds."

"They ain't got any G-d D----d minds!" he said. "Hold him there, Dick. Stall it some way. Just give me a couple of hours—an hour. You do that, and I'll appreciate it. I'll appreciate it, very much, Dick."

"I'll certainly do my best, Mr. Kossmeyer" I said." I can't make no promises, but—"

He banged up the phone.

I went on back to the booth where Charlie Alt was.

He looked at me, looking sort of sore, an then he kind of laughed. "Halvers?" he said.

"Halvers?" I said. "Halvers on what, Charlie?"

"Halvers on what you get from Kossmeyer," he said. "H---, it's only fair, Dick. I was going to call him myself if you hadn't got firsts on the phone. I'd've give you half if I'd called him."

Well, there was two schools of thought on that, if you follow my meaning. But there wasn't much else I could do so I said, well, all right, if he felt he was entitled to it.

"Kossy says we should stall," I said. "We stall an hour or maybe two until he can get hold of some judge for a habeas, he'll appreciate it very much."

"Kossy's all right," Charlie said. "He's one good Jew if you ask me."

"What you got to say a thing like that for?" I said. "He can't help it if he's a Jew, can he? What's wrong with being a Jew?"

"H---," Charlie said. "What you snapping me up for? I say something nice about him, and you snap me up."

"Well," I said.

"You'd better watch yourself, Dick," he said. "You go around acting like that and people will think maybe you're part Jew yourself."

"Like who maybe will think that?" I said. "Anyway, I'd a lot rather be a Jew than some certain other people I know, if you follow my meaning."

"Yeah?" he said.

"Yes," I said.

He sat and frowned at me a minute or two, and then he picked up the menu.

"H---," he said, looking at the menu. "I don't know why you got to get sore, Dick. Didn't I say Kossy was a good friend of mine? Didn't I say he was a hundred per cent gentleman and the best lawyer in town? H---, that's nothing to get sore about."

"Well, all right," I said. "I guess maybe I misunderstood you."

"I tell you what I think I'll do," he said. "I'd just as soon skip the peas. That makes two thirty-five instead of two-fifty."

"I'd just as soon, too," I said. "We can get some extra bread for nothing if we want."

We gave our order to the waiter, told him to make the steaks extra well done. The d.a. telephoned when we'd just started eating, so the waiter told him we was eating and he said to tell us to get a move on.

"What the h---?" Charlie said. "We ain't supposed to eat any more?"

"That's what I say," I said. "I guess maybe we can't order our steaks the way we want 'em."

"What you think Kossy will give us, Dick?" he said.

"Well . . . twenty apiece, maybe," I said. "Probably fifty if we can stall until he comes up with the habeas."

Charlie kind of whistled. "Fif-ty bucks! What I can't do with that! You really think he will, Dick?"

"Why not?" I said. "I got fifty from Kossy two or three times. Things that wasn't as much trouble as this."

"Yeah," he said. "But there wasn't anyone else in on it. He didn't have to pay no one but you."

"He didn't, huh?" I winked at him. "Vas you dere, Charlie?"

"Wow! Fifty bucks!" Charlie said. "I tell you something, Dick. I'll do something if you will. What you say we each drop an extra quarter for Who Flung Dung?"

(The waiter's name was Hop Lee, but Charlie always called him Hopalong or Who Flung Dung or something like that. Just kidding, you understand.)

"You mean we give him fifty cents besides the thirty cents?" I said. "Almost a dollar tip?"

"What the h---?" Charlie said. "We can afford it, can't we?"

"Well, I don't know," I said. "Suppose we can't stall long enough. We maybe can't get away with it."

"We'll get away with it," Charlie said. "I'll knock Clinton down and set on him if I have to."

"Well, all right," I said. "You leave an extra two-bits and I will. But I'd feel a lot more comfortable about it if I had that fifty bucks in my pocket."

"Fifty bucks!" Charlie said. "Boy, oh, boy! You still want to make a deal on that Smith & Wesson, Dick?"

"I'll sell it," I said. "I ain't taking any old beat-up Colt in trade."

"Beat up?" he said. "And I guess that old Smith & Wesson ain't beat up! I guess you bought it brand new from Mr. Smith and Wesson instead of taking it off of that nigger highjacker."

"I wouldn't say anything about me taking things off of people, Charlie," I said, "if you follow my meaning."

"Well, don't go running down my Colt all the time," he said. "People hear you knocking it all the time, I never will get rid of it. I had two or three trades worked up, and someone hears a knock on it—I ain't saying it came from you, now—and the deal falls through."

"Look, Charlie," I said. "Irregardless of what you may have heard to the contrary, I have never at any time or place knocked that Colt to anyone. On the contrary, Charlie, and I can prove it. Dusty Kramer, over on city vice, he came up to me the other day and said, frankly, what was my honest opinion, and I said frankly I didn't see how a man could go wrong on a good Colt. I said you asked for my honest opinion, and there it is. You see yourself a good Colt at the right price and you better grab it."

"Well," Charlie said. "I didn't say you knocked it, Dick. I didn't think you'd do a thing like that."

"You know why I don't want to take in a trade," I said. "I've explained the situation to you several times, Charlie. I got a Colt and I got a Smith & Wesson, and getting rid of the Smith & Wesson, I still have the Colt. I don't want another one, two Colts, even if it ain't all beat up."

"This is my last offer," Charlie said. "I'll swap you the Colt and fifteen dollars, no, twenty dollars. That's my last offer, Dick, take it or leave it."

"You just made yourself a deal, mister," I said.

"I'll pay you tomorrow," he said, "just as soon as we get the dough from Kossmeyer."

"Well, all right," I said, "but if it's no dough, no deal. I got to have the cash on the line, Charlie."

"You'll get it," he said. "We'll stall that Clinton if we have to hogtie him."

We finished our steak and potatoes, and had some pie and coffee. Then, we had second coffees and someway the waiter didn't charge us for them, so we left that money for him, too. Another twenty cents with the eighty. An even dollar tip. Me and Charlie kind of wanted to be around when he picked it up, see how he'd act, you know, but he was busy with some other tables and we figured we'd better be getting back.

Practically everyone had been gone from the courthouse when we left, and everyone was gone now. I mean all the other offices was closed up tight but the d.a.'s, and even the elevator boy had gone home. All the lights was off but just a few little ones, and we practically had to feel our way up the stairs and down the corridor.

We got to the d.a.'s office, the first one you go into I mean that's got the railing running down the center and went on through the gate. Charlie was in the lead and I was right on his heels, and when we stopped all of a sudden I piled right into him.

"Excuse me, Charlie," I said.

"Shh," he said. "G-d d--n!"

He jerked his head at the door of the witness room, and I listened. I heard the d.a. say something, and then I heard the kid say something. There was a sound about it I didn't like one little bit, and I could tell that Charlie didn't like it one little bit either.

He turned around and looked at me, and I looked at him. I could tell he was thinking the same thought I was.

"Well, Charlie," I said. "I guess them was just about the most expensive steaks we'll ever eat."

"G-d D--n," he said. "S-n of a b---h!"

"I guess we should've et 'em rare," I said.

"Shh," he said. "Listen, G-d D--n it!"

So we listened:

"Now, Bob, you want to tell the truth, don't you? Do you want to tell the truth or do you want to go on lying?"

"Yes! I mean, no, I don't want to! I mean I'm not I don't k-know I—"

"You don't know what the truth is, do you, Bob? Isn't that what you mean? You'd rather tell the truth than to tell a lie, wouldn't you? If I helped you out and told you what the truth was, would you tell it or would you tell a lie?"

"Y-yes—no! I don't know! Y-you got me all m-mix—"

"You didn't mean to kill that girl, did you, Bob? Did you? Just answer yes or no; did you or didn't you mean to kill her?"

"I . . . n-no."

"If you didn't mean to, then it would be an accident wouldn't it? Isn't that right, Bob?"

"I—I—I g-guess."

"You didn't go near the golf course, did you? Well, how do you know it wasn't a half a mile? Did you measure it? How do you know it wasn't a mile or two miles or . . ."

"Because I told you an' told—"

"But that was a lie, remember? You wanted me to tell you the truth, because you'd rather tell the truth than tell a lie. Isn't that right?"

"I—I don't know! I'm telling the truth!"

"Fine. Of course, you are. You're beginning to remember, get straightened out, and now you're telling the truth. You're a good boy, Bob. I knew it all the time. You liked little Josie. You might have got frightened and lost your head, everyone does that, but you liked her. You wouldn't have killed her accidentally and then just wandered on off to the golf course as if nothing had happened. You don't want me to think you'd do that, do you?"

"N-no . . ."

"How many times did you and she do it, Bob?"

"J-just—"

"Sure, but once can be several, can't it? It could be, couldn't it, Bob? You know, several times together?"

"I d-don't . . . WHAT YOU WANT ME TO SAY? WHAT YOU—"

"Oh, I can't tell you what to say, Bob. That wouldn't be fair. Now, if you want me to help you remember—tell it in the right words so people will know you're a fine boy and it was all just a mistake like anyone might make . . . Is that what you mean, Bob? You want me to help you, put it in the right words, so—"

"Y-Y-YES!"

Charlie Alt yanked the cigar out of his mouth, and flung it on the floor.

"G-d D--n," he said. "Good-bye fifty bucks!"

i. kossmeyer 10

I walked around my desk, and got right in front of Mrs. Talbert. I let my hands dangle, kangaroo fashion, pulled the corners of my mouth down and started fluttering my eyelids. It was a pretty good imitation of her, if I do say so.

"Now, this is the way you look, Mrs. Talbert," I said. "This is the way you sound . . . Wheeoo, yoweee, boo-hoo, blab-blab, honestly, actually, really, I can't stand it, yickety-yickety-yoo, blah blah blah."

It took her completely by surprise. She couldn't make up her mind whether to laugh or get sore.

"W-well—well, honestly!" she began. "I—"

"You see?" I grinned at her. "There you go again."

Well, she was pretty red-faced for a moment, and then suddenly she burst out laughing. Talbert gave her a startled look. I don't imagine he'd heard her laugh like that in years. I don't imagine he could have pulled a gag or a bit of clowning if his life depended on it.

"Now, that's better," I said. "Aren't you ashamed of yourself, Mrs. Talbert? A pretty young woman like you running around like a hen with its head off. Cackling and gabbling around about everything you know and ten times as much that you don't. Weeping and wailing and yackety-yak bloo-blahing. Why, if you weren't so pretty I'd turn you over my knee and paddle you."

She blushed, and giggled. "Why, Mr. Kossmeyer! You awful—"

"Well, all right," I said. "You be a good girl from now on. No more gabbing to anyone. No more pitching the dirt to or about anyone. No more bloo-booing and boohooing and all around nuttiness. We need friends, all we can get, understand? We need to act confident. You want to talk to someone you come and see me. We'll give your old man a sleeping pill, and throw a wingding."

"Mr. Kossmeyer!" she simpered. "You're just simply *terrible!*"

"You'll think I'm terrible," I said, "if you give me any more trouble. Now, scram on out of here while your husband and I have a little talk. Go out and talk to my secretary. Tell her I said to order you up the biggest coke in town or I won't hold her on my knee any more."

She went out giggling and blushing, and the poor old biddy actually twitched her butt at me. I drew the chair she'd been sitting in up in front of Talbert.

"All right," I said. "She needed that. That was for laughs. This isn't. How much money can you raise?"

"Well—uh—" He hesitated cautiously. "How much will you need?"

"More than I'll get out of you," I said. "So make it light on me."

He frowned, uncomfortably. He just wasn't used to doing business this way. "Well, I, uh—I just don't know. If you could give me some idea—"

"Look," I said. "Look, Mr. Talbert. You've already placed me under a very serious handicap. If you'd done what you should have instead of giving way to your emotions and losing your head, you wouldn't be here and your boy wouldn't be where he is."

"I know," he said. "I don't know why I—"

I cut him off. "Forget it. It's over and done, so let's get back to the subject. All I ask of my clients is that they pay their own way as far as they can. You tell me what you can do, and we'll let it go at that."

"Well," he said. "A—uh—thousand dollars?"

I nodded, staring at him. "All right, Mr. Talbert. You know what you can do."

"Will you . . . ?" He looked down at the floor. "I wouldn't want to feel that Bob wasn't—that the money—"

"It won't make a bit of difference," I said. "I'll do just as much for a thousand as I would for ten thousand. Or a hundred. I always do my best. That's all I ask my clients to do."

"'I've got a house," he said. "A pretty good equity in it. I kind of hoped that—"

"Many of my clients don't have so much as a suit of clothes, Mr. Talbert. Not even the price of their next meal."

"I'll get as much as I can," he said. "Whatever I can get, well, I'll be glad to do it."

"Good," I said, "Get busy on it right away."

He looked a little let down. Gratitude yet, he expected! I was putting the blocks to him, and I wasn't even being nice about it. I tricked him and kicked him at the same time.

That was the way he felt, and why the hell I let it bother me I don't know, because I've never had a client who didn't feel exactly the same way. Enough: they don't know what that is. But too much—that's simple. Too much is what they pay you. And it's still too much if they don't pay anything. You're getting all that free publicity, see? Worth plenty of dough to you. And I've actually had 'em try to collect!

"Well, I believe that's about all," I said. "If you want to run along now, get busy on that money . . ."

"But—" He got to his feet slowly, frowning—"But what are you going to do, Mr. Kossmeyer?"

I shrugged. "Whatever is necessary, Mr. Talbert."

"Well, I . . . I just wondered. I kind of wanted to know."

"That's it," I said. "Whatever is necessary."

I smiled and nodded at him. He turned toward the door, hesitated. And then it came, the old, old question:

Mumbled and jumbled and garbled, as it almost always is, but still the same old question.

"Mr. Talbert," I said. "I never think but one thing. I not only think it but I believe it. As an officer of the court, I'm professionally and morally obliged to. Otherwise, I would be an accomplice in perjury and the obstruction of justice. I have had no guilty clients, Mr. Talbert. To the best of my knowledge and belief, they are always innocent."

"Well," he said, shamefaced. "Of course, I was sure that—"

"'Go right on being sure," I said.

"It'll be all right, won't it? You'll—he'll be cleared?"

"My clients are very seldom convicted," I said. "The real trouble often comes later."

"Oh?" He blinked at me. "How do you—"

"All the judges aren't in the courtroom," I said. "So never stop being sure. Never let the boy know that you're not sure."

"It's so mixed up," he said, absently. "It's all so mixed up. I know he couldn't have done it. I know they made him sign that confession. Why, you look at it this way, Mr. Kossmeyer. I know it maybe looks funny, but—"

"Certainly," I said. "You're absolutely right, Mr. Talbert."

I grabbed him by the hand, shook it and shoved him out the door.

. . . I waited a couple of days before I dropped in on the district attorney. I had a few things I wanted to take care of first, and I thought it would be a good idea to let him stew a while. As I saw it, he'd be expecting me right away; it would worry him when I didn't show. I hoped, of course, that he might get worried enough to come to me. But I hadn't got any other breaks on the deal, and I didn't get that one.

"Why, Kossy," he said, jumping up from his desk. "This is a pleasant surprise! Sit down, sit down. How have you been, anyway?"

"Aaaah," I said. "Nothing new, Clint. Same old sixes and sevens."

"What's this I hear about your name being put up for a circuit court appointment? I was just going to call and ask if I could be of help in any way. Write a few letters or say a word or two in the right places. I believe I have some small influence and—"

"Well, that's very kind of you, Clint," I said. "But, no, I guess there's nothing to it. My God, what would I do on the Federal bench! I'd be lost, y'know. I wouldn't know how to act."

"Oh, now," he murmured. "I wouldn't say that, Kossy."

"What they really need is someone like you," I said. "Someone with a lot of dignity and a broad background in public service. By the way, I suppose you know you're considered also?"

He was completely astonished. But *completely*. He said so himself.

"Why—why, Kossy," he said. "I hardly know what to say. Not that I'd stand the slightest chance, of course, but . . ."

"I don't see why not," I said. "It seems to me you might stand a very excellent chance. If I withdraw, swing such small support as I may have over to you, why—"

"Well," he said, "I couldn't ask you to do that. I'd appreciate it, of course, but—"

"You don't have to ask," I said. "I'd simply be doing it as a matter of civic duty. After all, if you can make the financial sacrifices entailed in accepting the appointment, I certainly should be willing to say a word here and there."

"Well, he said. "That's certainly very nice of you. It's nice of you to feel that way."

He sat looking down at his desk for a moment, rocking back and forth in his swivel chair. He sighed, shook his head, and looked up.

"Kossy," he said. "You dirty son-of-a-bitch."

"I meant it," I said. "Just that and nothing more. And no strings attached." And I *did* mean it.

"I know," he said. "That's what makes you such a son-of-a-bitch. It's indecent, God damn it. If you had a spark of humanity in you, you'd offer me an outright bribe."

I laughed, and he joined in. Rather tiredly, I thought. He pushed a cigar box across the desk, held a match for me. His hand trembled, and he drew it away quickly.

"Now, about young Talbert," he said. "I assume you're here in his interests? Well, I'm willing to do everything I can, Kossy. The boy is more to be pitied than condemned, in my opinion. He's made a tragic mistake, a very serious one, but I can't regard him as a criminal in the ordinary sense of the word. I—"

"And of course, he's been very cooperative," I said. "We can't overlook that, can we, Clint?"

He creaked back and forth in his chair, his hands folded on his stomach, his eyes studying me gravely. I folded my hands on my stomach, rocked back and forth in my chair and frowned at him. He scowled, and leaned forward.

"That has all the earmarks of a very nasty insinuation, Kossy. Are you implying that the boy's constitutional rights were violated?"

"Of course not," I said. "I can't even think all those big words without getting tangled up. All I'm saying is that you sweated that kid until he didn't know his ass from an adding machine. He'd have sworn that he killed Christ if you told him to."

"Well," he said, "that's one murder we didn't have to inquire about."

I laughed and said he was certainly right. Someone laughed and said he was certainly right. I took the cigar out of my mouth, and studied it. And studied it. Damn him, the dirty stinking—. No, he hadn't meant what he had said. But he *had* said it. Damn him, damn him, da—

"Kossy," he said, "that was a rotten thing to say. I'm thoroughly ashamed. Please forgive me."

"What the hell?" I said. "I needled you pretty hard. Anyway, you didn't say anything. I wasn't even listening to you. Now—"

"Kossy, my friend. I—"

"I said you didn't say anything!" I said. "Get me? I wasn't listening to you. I—I—God damn, you call *this* a cigar? You ought to serve corned beef with it."

"All right, Kossy," he smiled. "Okay, boy."

"Now, getting back to this alleged confession, Clint. I'll tell you how I feel about it. The boy didn't have an alibi; he was known to have had relations with the girl. All in all, and with the newspapers turning on the heat—that's one thing I can't figure out, incidentally—"

"Oh, the *newspapers*," he shrugged. "I never pay any attention to 'em, Kossy."

"Well, that just about makes you unique," I said. "At any rate, you jumped to the entirely erroneous conclusion that the boy was guilty and you felt justified in, uh, urging him to admit it. Insisting that he admit it until he couldn't hold out any longer. You were just doing your job, as you saw it, but—"

"You're dead wrong, Kossy. Naturally, I talked to the boy at some length, but there was certainly no duress involved. He was as entirely free to maintain his innocence as he was to admit his guilt. It's his own confession, told of his own free will in his own words."

"That's what you believe," I said. "You couldn't prosecute him if you didn't believe it. But take a tip from me, Clint. Don't go into court with that confession. You go into court with that, and I'll rip you to pieces."

"Oh, *well*," he said. "Of course, if you want to make a jury case out of it, have the boy treated like some hardened criminal . . ."

"What did you have in mind?" I said.

"Well, I certainly didn't contemplate anything like that, Kossy. Now, he's your client, of course, and I wouldn't want to urge any course of action upon you. But I thought you and I might just talk it over quietly with one of the juvenile justices, someone like old mother Meehan, and I'm sure her honor would give very serious consideration to any recommendations."

"Such as?" I said.

"Well"—he pursed his lips—"state industrial? Until he attains his majority?"

"Huh-uh," I said.

"We-el. You may well be right, Kossy. I'm inclined to feel that you are. If the boy wasn't responsible for what he did, and, frankly, how can you hold a mere child responsible, why he certainly shouldn't be punished. He isn't bad; he's only sick. He's sorely in need of treatment. Perhaps a brief stay in one of our state hospitals—I see no reason at all why he shouldn't be fully restored and ready to return to society within, oh, possibly eighteen months; well, a year, then. Or even nine months. I believe I can guarantee an outside maximum of nine months. I believe I can explain to the court that it's largely a matter of rest and quiet, having time for reflection and—"

"Huh-uh," I said. "Absolutely no."

"You name it, then. What's your best offer, Kossy?"

"Complete dismissal. Unqualified exoneration. The boy was excited, overly tired. He didn't realize what he was saying."

"Nonsense. No, siree. No, by God!"

"That's it," I said. "And, Clint, that still leaves it plenty bad for the boy. It leaves it lousy for him and his parents. If he walked out of the place this minute, he'd still be getting the rawest deal a kid could get. He'll suffer for it the rest of his life. Think of it, Clint! Think of what it's going to mean to him at school, and after he leaves school, starts looking for a job, or when he meets some nice gal and wants to get married. . . . Would you want a child of yours to run around with a kid who was the prime suspect in a rape-murder case? Would you want him on your payroll? Would you want your daughter to marry him? Would you want to associate with him yourself? Don't say it, Clint. Don't tell me people will forget. They'll forget, all right—that he wasn't convicted. It's like the old song: the words are ended but the melody lingers on. And it'll get louder and uglier wherever he goes, whatever he does, as long as he lives."

"That's what you say. I feel otherwise. Mind you, now" —he held up a hand—"mind you, my mind isn't closed on the matter. You show me something, just anything at all that might cast a reasonable doubt on his guilt, and I'll be most happy to consider it. You'll find me unusually receptive, Kossy. I'll be just as pleased as you are. But, hell, I can't—"

"Let him go, Clint," I said. "It'll still be bad enough."

"So? Aren't you being remiss then in asking me to discharge him? Shouldn't you prove him innocent beyond any shadow of a doubt? Is anything less fair to him?"

"Clint," I said. "How many of these sex murderers are ever run down? You can't type them on *modus operandi*; they're not peculiar to any particular group or class. They look like you and me and everyone else, and they *are* you and me and everyone else. The corner grocer and the chain-store executive, the bum and the big business man, the choir singer and the dice hustler, the minister, the prize fighter, the guy who mows your lawn and the guy who—"

"Kossy. I think you must have misunderstood me. I said nothing about your producing the guil—another suspect. That isn't what I said at all."

"Isn't that about what it amounts to?"

"Not at all. We have evidence of his guilt. I merely pointed out that without something to dispel that evidence, some reasonably concrete proof of innocence, my hands were tied. You can see that, Kossy. You can't conscientiously expect me to drop the case. It wouldn't be fair to the boy."

He reached for the cigar box again, raised his eyebrows at me. I shook my head.

"I'll get him off, Clint," I said. "I'll get a verdict or a dismissal. You ain't got a God damn thing but the confession, and I'll rip it to pieces. It'll have more holes in it than a whores' convention."

He laughed. "Ah, Kossy. I'll bet you do take my hide off, at that. However, I don't think I'd count too much on getting him off."

"Let him go, Clint. I know you want to."

"I can't, Kossy. It's simply unthinkable."

"Let him go. Give him a clean bill of health. It'll still be bad, but it's better than anything else."

"I can't. Understand me, Kossy? I can't!"

I hadn't actually expected him to. Just hoped. His case might not be too strong, but it was stronger than mine, and with all the newspapers raising hell, keeping the deal spotlighted . . .

No, he couldn't do it.

I picked up my briefcase from the floor, and stood up. "All right, Clint," I said. "I guess that takes care of everything for the present. Now, if I can have a little chat with the boy . . ."

"Certainly, certainly." He punched a button on his desk. "I'll tell the matron to clear out and see that you're not disturbed. Incidentally, I think you'll see that we've done everything possible to make things pleasant for Bob."

"I'm sure of it," I said. "Now, about that civil court

appointment, Clint. I'm really going to pour the coal on that. I'm only sorry I didn't get busy on it sooner."

"Kossy," he said. "I . . . well, I just don't know what to say. I don't know how to thank you."

"Nuts," I said. "Thank me? You don't even know anything about it."

"Why don't we have lunch some time soon? I'll give you a ring."

"You'd better let me call you," I said. "You know how it is. I never know what's going to crop up until the very last minute."

"What about Sunday? You're not busy on Sunday. Come out for dinner and spend the afternoon with us. We haven't had a good talk in a long time."

"Thanks," I said. "I'd love to. Give me a raincheck, will you? Some other time? I'm kind of tied up for the next few weeks."

His smile faded. He turned and stared out the window, spoke with his back turned to me. He was thinking of that "Christ murder" remark.

"You'll never forget that, will you?" he said. "You can't forget it."

"Forget what?" I said.

"I don't know why I said it, Kossy. You know I'm no anti-Semite. I'd give anything in the world if I hadn't said it. I know there's no use in saying I'm sorry, but—"

"Sorry?" I said. "What about? What are you supposed to have said? I didn't hear you say a thing, Clint."

i. kossmeyer 11

The kid seemed quite contented and at peace with the
world. They usually are that way after a hard sweat-
ing. They've been down through hell and come up the
other side, and they're still right there on the brink, but it
seems nice. No more questions. No more loud voices and
bright lights. No more scowls and frowns. Nothing but
smiles and friendliness, quiet and rest. You've done the
"right thing," see? And possibly it *is* the right thing, but
it's still wrong. Guilty or innocent, it's wrong. It's difficult
to place a rope around a man's neck: the law, slowly
evolving through the centuries, winding its way up
through dungeons and torture chambers, emerging at last
into the sunlight, intended it to be difficult. Now, in suf-
fering the law to be put aside, in placing the rope where
others could not place it, in retreating to the evil chaos of
no-law, you have done the "right thing," and you are
rewarded for it. And so, too, are the men like Clinton
rewarded, men who achieve the surface right through the
depthless wrong. Convictions: those are the sole criteria
in judging the Clintons. For the law has changed, but people have not. They are still lingering back in the shadows;
thumbs turned down on the fallen, hustling wood for the
witch-burner, donning their bedsheets and boots at the
first smell of blood.

. . . There was a portable radio going in the window. The
table was loaded down with fruit and candy bars and
potato chips, and he had a stack of comic books two feet
high. He was reading one of the comic books when I went
in, turning the pages with his finger tips since he had a
coke in one hand and a banana in the other.

He went on reading it, answering me absently, apparently unconcerned with what had happened and what might happen. He was all right now. Miraculously, he had been snatched up from the abyss. He did not want to leave the present, to look back from it or beyond it.

He inquired about his folks: why hadn't they come to see him.

I said that they'd wanted to, but I'd felt they'd better not. They were badly upset. It would be hard on everyone concerned.

"Well," he said, idly. "I guess maybe that's right. I guess maybe they better wait."

He turned a page of the comic book. He read it, the coke and banana moving alternately to his mouth, and turned another one.

"Wait for what, Bob?" I said. "Until you serve your sentence or until you get out of the nut house?"

"What?" he said.

"Listen to me, Bob," I said. "I—*Bob!*"

"Yeah?" He frowned, fretfully, without looking up. "I'm listening, ain't I?"

I snatched the comic book out of his hand and threw it across the room. I brushed the banana into the wastebasket, and tossed the coke after it.

He said, "Hey! What'd you do—"

"Shut up!" I said. "I'm asking all the questions, get me? I ask the questions and you give the answers, and you have your mind on 'em when you do it. Do you understand that, Bob? I asked you if you understood that!"

Some of the vagueness went out of his eyes. He nodded sullenly, a little fearfully.

"All right," I said. "Question number one: why did you lie to me that first night I talked to you?"

"Lie? I didn't tell you any lie."

"Who did you lie to? Come on, spit it out! You told me you didn't kill Josie Eddleman and you told the district attorney that you did. Now which was the lie?"

"Well, I—Mr. Clinton said—"

"To hell with what Mr. Clinton said. I don't give a fast-day fart for what he said. Did you lie to me? Did you kill that girl?"

He shook his head. "Huh-uh. O' course, I didn't."

"You lied to Mr. Clinton, then. If you didn't lie to me you lied to him. Isn't that right, Bob? Both stories couldn't have been the truth. If you told me the truth, you didn't tell him the truth. Isn't that right?"

He hesitated.

I said, "Well, how about it?"

"'Well, uh, you see"—his eyes wavered—"I was kind of mixed up. I wanted to tell him the truth, but I was mixed up. So he said, well, maybe it was this way an' that way, how did I know it wasn't, and maybe it could have been. And I said, maybe it was, I guess it was. I was all mixed up, and he wasn't. So I told him the truth like he said."

"I see," I said. "You told him you killed Josie, and that was the truth, and you told me you didn't kill her and that was the truth."

"Uh-huh. That's—"

I slapped him across the mouth.

I swung my hand back and forth, slapping him palm and backhand.

The matron pounded on the door and rushed in. I told her to beat it.

"I'm slapping hell out of a client," I said, "and I don't want to be disturbed."

"I'm going to report this to Mr. Clinton!"

"You do that," I said. "Take your time going and don't hurry back."

She slammed out, and of course she didn't return. Clint knew what I was doing; he couldn't object to it. With slight variations and with, naturally, a contrary purpose, I was doing exactly what he'd done.

I led the boy over to the sink, telling him, hell, not to cry: I was just trying to be his friend and he'd thank me for it some day. I helped him to wash his face, kidding and joshing until he began to smile a little.

"That's swell," I said. "That's my boy. Now we'll start getting somewhere. We're not mixed up any more, now, are we?"

"N-No, sir."

"You didn't kill Josie, did you?"

"No, sir. I guess I— No, sir."

"You told me the truth. What you told Mr. Clinton was not the truth."

"Yes, sir."

"You were out at the golf course at noon. Before noon and for some time afterwards."

"Yes, sir."

"Did Mr. Clinton make any promises to you for giving him that confession? Did he say something like, well, you tell us you killed Josie and we'll let you go?"

"Well"—he hesitated—"I kind of felt like he did. He said that if I'd do the right thing, he would; that he knew I didn't really mean to do it and it was just a mistake and he didn't believe in punishing anyone for—"

"But he didn't make you any outright promise?"

"No—not exactly, I guess. I mean it kind of seemed like he did, but . . ."

I nodded and unstrapped my briefcase.

He said, "Mr. Kossmeyer. What will they—?"

"Nothing," I said. "They won't do a damned thing. Just keep telling the truth, and everything will be all right."

I got the briefcase open, and took out a thick sheaf of photographs. I spread them out on the lounge in three rows and nodded to him.

"These are aerial photographs, Bob. They were taken from a helicopter. They begin there at the trestle, the canyon, near your home and move in a bee-line to the golflinks. In other words, they show the area you passed through on the way to the links . . ."

"Yes, sir?" he said.

"Now, of course, being pictures, everything is considerably reduced—bear that in mind—but it's all there. All the trees and telephone poles and other landmarks. You look at them and show me the route you followed as well as you remember it."

He bent over the pictures. After a moment, he turned and looked at me.

"They ain't—they're not in the right order. You want me to unmix 'em?"

"Are you sure?" I said. "Well, yes, you straighten them out, Bob."

The pictures were actually one picture, one long strip photograph which I'd chopped into sections. I'd mixed those sections up deliberately.

He had them straightened out within two minutes.

That didn't prove anything, of course, but it was a little something, some satisfaction to me, at least. It established that he had been through the area very recently.

I gave him a pencil, and he pointed out the route he had followed. He did it very quickly. Maybe—I thought—a little too quickly?

"Did you always go this same way, Bob? Down this little slope and up the next one and so on?"

"Well . . ." He scratched his head.

"You went pretty much the same way each time, right? That's how you remember it so well."

He studied my face doubtfully, cautiously. He wet his lips.

"What"—he edged back a step—"what you want me to say, Mr. Kossmeyer?"

"Just the truth, Bob. Whatever the truth is, that's what I want you to tell me."

"Well . . . I guess not, then. I mean, I guess I just went that way that day."

"Fine," I said, soothingly. "That's the truth, and that's all I want. Now, let's see. Let's see if I remember as well as you do. You were pretty excited that day. You weren't thinking about scenery, just walking fast without looking to right or left. That's right, isn't it, Bob? I've got it right? Then tell me—just the truth—tell me how you remember the way you went so well."

"Well . . ." He swallowed noisily. "Maybe I don't remember. Maybe—if you don't want me to say I—"

"Bob," I said. "Listen to me, kid. I'm on your side. I'm your friend. I'm like a doctor, see? You know how a doctor has to hurt a guy sometimes for his own good. Well, that's me, that's what I was doing a moment ago. You understand that. Sure you do. You re a smart boy, and a damned fine one. So—so just keep right on telling me the truth. Tell me how you remember."

"Well. I don't exactly remember. I just kind of know."

"Yes?"

"It kind of comes back to me. I wasn't noticing anything, hardly, at the time. But now I sort of do. I mean, I kind of know—I don't exactly remember, but I know."

"Swell," I said. "You're doing fine, Bob."

"Most of the time, usually, it'd been some other day, I'd kind of wander around. I'd maybe wander off to look at a rabbit hole or something, or maybe I'd try to jump across a little gully or see if I could hit a telephone pole with a rock or—well, that's the way I'd usually do. But that day, I just wasn't interested in anything like that. I just went right straight ahead, just the straightest I could go and—"

"Sure, you did!" I said. "Naturally! That's exactly what you would do, what anyone would do. That's swell, Bob, that's really swell."

No, it didn't prove anything. It wasn't nearly enough to swing Clint around, or to go to trial with. Still, it would help . . . a little. It was something to build on. It sounded so plausible, so authentic, you know, not the kind of thing a kid could invent on the spur of the moment. If he'd stick to it, if it was true, if he just wasn't beating his brains out to please me for fear of getting them beat out. . . .

I wished I hadn't roughed him. I wished to God I hadn't. And, yet, there'd been nothing else to do. He'd had to be snapped out of it fast. Hell, he might have taken days to do it by himself—if he ever did it—and we didn't have days. Anyway, I didn't. . . . Only one client, I had? I got forever to spend with one client? You should live so long, Kossmeyer!

I opened a coke for him, and took one myself. I kidded with him some more, did a little clowning, made him laugh a few times. He seemed pretty much at ease when we went back to the pictures. He answered my questions with only normal hesitation, telling the truth apparently without regard for how I might take it.

Yeah, that was an excavation there by that highline tower, but it had been there a long time. He didn't know why it was there unless they'd started to dig the hole for the tower in the wrong place, but he hadn't seen anyone working there. There hadn't been anyone around those towers since he didn't know when.

Yeah, that was a pasture, all right, those were some cows. But the house was way off over on the highway, several miles off. You had to be over by the highway to see it, and he hadn't been anywhere near.

Yeah, that was kind of a dump over there on the left; that is, it had been a dump. Now, though it was fenced in and it was against the law to dump anything there. Anyway, it was too far off from the way he'd gone. It was over on kind of an old country road that no one used any more.

Yeah, that was a pond. There were two or three of those little ponds. But there wasn't anything in them but maybe a few tadpoles. No one fished in 'em or swam in 'em or anything. He'd never seen anyone near them, so, well, he guessed there couldn't have been anyone that day.

No—well, yeah, he did take a smoke now and then, but just when someone had given him one. He never bought any. He hadn't left any butts lying around the spot where he'd sat killing time. Yeah, that was the place, right in there in those rocks. Yeah, the ground was pretty hard there, all right. Maybe there might be some footprints or something, but that wouldn't prove anything, would it? He might have made them some other day. . . . Yeah, he had this wrist-watch; he'd had that watch for, well, almost always. His Dad had bought it for him when they were in the city together, and . . . yeah, that's how he'd known the time. He hadn't asked anyone. There hadn't been anyone to ask. . . .

We came to the end of the pictures, but he rambled on a minute or two longer, talking about the watch and the time his Dad had bought it for him. Then, he looked at me, and the skin around his cheekbones seemed to tighten.

"I . . . I guess I'm not doing so well, am I?" he said.

"Nonsense," I said. "You're doing swell, Bob. You just keep it up and everything'll be fine."

"B-but—what'll Mr. Clinton do if we can't—"

"Frig Mr. Clinton," I said. "You ain't done a God damned thing, and they ain't going to do a God damned thing to you. Now, let's go back through these pictures, just for the hell of it and . . ."

We went through the pictures again. Except that he was a little slower with it, it was the same story.

I got up and paced around the room. He watched me, started to say something a couple of times, and I guess I cut him off pretty short.

I scraped the pictures up from the lounge and carried them over to the window. I held them up to the light, turned through them slowly.

Nothing. I'd taken him over every step of the way, and there was nothing. Nothing that might mean people—someone who could have seen him.

I came to the last picture, and I cursed out loud. Why couldn't he have gone on to the golf course? Why couldn't he have gone at least a little further down the bluff so that he might have been seen from the course? Why the hell did he have to stay back there in those God damned rocks when—

I let the pictures slide out of my hands, all but the last one. I held it up to the light, turning it this way and that, squinting at it.

"Bob," I said. "Come here! Hurry up, God damn it!"

"Y-Yes, sir." He came running like a dog. "Yes, Mr. Kossmeyer?"

"This little dark patch over here on the far right . . . see it? See where I'm pointing? Down in the bottom of that little swell of land—there in those weeds or bushes or whatever they are."

"Yes, sir. I see it."

"What is it? It looks like it might be a little clearing."

"Yes, sir. I guess maybe it is."

"Maybe?" I said. "Don't you know? You've wandered all over hell out there, looked at everything else within a ten mile radius, don't you know what this is?"

"Well, I—there was some colored people over there,

once, over that way, and this big old fat woman she looked pretty mean, so I figured I'd better stay away from there . . ."

He looked at me anxiously. I let out a groan. "You saw a— Wait a minute! You only saw her the one time, and yet you never went near there afterward?"

"W-Well, I guess it was more than that. I guess I've seen her pretty often, her and some colored kids."

"You guess! You must have, didn't you? Didn't you? When was the last time?"

"Well, I—I—"

"God," I said. "God in heaven! It must be a garden and you've seen people around it, and you didn't tell me about it! Don't you know they must live around there? Were you ever over in these woods? When was the last time you saw them—any of them?"

"N-Not—not very long ago, I guess. It kind of seems like it wasn't. Y-You see, I don't—didn't—try to see 'em. I mean, I get near there I always kind of look the other way, so that, well, they won't think I'm spying or anything. I kind of try to circle around, and pretend like—"

"When was the last time you saw them? I know. You pretended not to look over that way and maybe you circled around, but you'd damned near've had to see them if they were around. You'd know they were there even without looking. When was it? A week ago, two weeks? Four days? That day, the day you—"

"Y-Yes, sir," he stammered. "It was that day, I guess. That's when it was, yes, sir! I remember now it was that day, Mr. Kossmeyer. I—"

"Are you sure? Are you *sure*, Bob?"

I grabbed him by the shoulders and shook him.

Then, I managed to get hold of myself, and I let go and stood back.

"I'm sorry," I said. "Don't pay me any mind, Bob. You know how it is when a guy gets excited."

"Yes, sir." He eyed me watchfully. "That's all right, Mr. Kossmeyer."

"Now, it doesn't make a bit of difference, see? If you saw

them, fine; if you didn't see them, fine. Just tell me the truth. Either way it'll be all right."

He knew better than that. He said, "I saw them. Maybe I didn't actually see them but I knew they were there. Some of 'em were there."

"Bob," I said. "I—well, tell me this, Bob. Right from the beginning I've tried to get you to remember if you saw anyone or passed anyone or talked to anyone who might give you an alibi for the time of the murder. I tried that first night I talked to you; I've gone back and forth through these pictures today, trying to. And I'm sure various other people tried to, Mr. Clinton and the detectives and the newspaper men. And you've maintained all along that there wasn't anyone, that you couldn't remember anyone. Now, you suddenly tell me—and I'm sure you wouldn't deliberately represent—now you tell me that—"

"W-Well," he faltered, "you don't want me to say so, I won't. If you say I didn't, well, maybe I didn't."

I mopped my face. "I *do* want you to say so, Bob, but only if it is the truth, if you're sure, that is. That's why I'm asking how you happen to remember now when you couldn't before. Just to make sure, see?"

He wet his lips again, looked down uneasily at the floor.

"Yes, Bob? How do you happen to remember? Why do you remember now when you didn't remember before now?"

"Well, I—I guess I was trying not to remember. You know how it is, something you're kind of afraid of but you can't do anything about, so you try to act like it isn't there. So—well, that's kind of the way it was with me and them. All those colored people, and just me by myself and no one else around. I tried to shut 'em out of my mind, and I guess I did. . . ."

I nodded. That took care of part of the question. It sounded reasonable—as, of course, we both wanted it to.

"Go on, Bob," I said. "You made yourself believe they weren't there. You convinced yourself that they weren't. Now, how do you remember they were?"

"Well"—his eyes clouded—"well, I guess it was something you said, the way you acted or something. It kind of scared me out of not remembering, sort of reminded me of them. I—I don't mean you're like them, o'course, but—"

"It's all right," I said. "Don't apologize. Go on."

"Well, I remembered they yelled at me, too. Cursed and yelled at me. When you started to—well, you know—well, it came back to me that they'd cursed and yelled."

"They'd never done that before?"

"Huh-uh."

"You'd gone by there day after day, they'd seen you day after day, and they'd never done anything like that before?"

"Huh-uh. . . . Well, maybe that one other time, back when I first noticed that place and that big old colored woman just stood and looked at me. Maybe she said something that day."

" But that was a long time ago. After that, they never did anything like that afterwards until four days ago?"

"Uh-huh."

"No," I said. "Not uh-huh, Bob. Uh-huh isn't enough. I've got to know why—"

"Well, I guess maybe it was the way I was acting. Just walking straight and not trying to keep out of their way or anything. Kind of acting like I didn't give a darn. I guess they must've thought I was sort of daring 'em."

Well, that too sounded reasonable. It all fitted together, perfectly. . . . Just the way we wanted it to.

I began gathering up the pictures and putting them in my briefcase.

"All right, Bob," I said. "That's fine. Of course, you realize I'll have to find these colored people and talk to them. They'll have to verify your story."

"Yeah?" he said. "Yeah, I guess so."

"I'll have to do it, Bob. They'll have to verify it, swear that it's true. It won't do us any good if they don't. In fact, if you should be mistaken, it might hurt us a great deal."

"Well," he said, sullenly, "I can't help what they say. I 'spect they'll probably say I wasn't there just to be mean.

They act like pretty mean people, an' that's what they'll probably do."

"Bob," I said, "look at me."

"What for? I'm lookin' at you, ain't I?"

"Look at me."

He looked up. He held my eyes stubbornly for a moment. Then, his face crumpled and he began to cry.

"W-What you want me to say?" he sobbed. "What you want me t-to say, anyhow . . . ? M-Maybe I didn't. Maybe I—I—You don't want m-me to say so, I won't. . . ."

. . . I parked my car on the road at the foot of the bluff, and climbed up to the top. I found the garden, a few rows of browning corn with withered sweet-potato and stringbean vines wound round the stalks. I found a path, and followed it down into the woods.

Their house, their dwelling, rather, had been assembled from packing boxes, scraps of sheet-iron, flattened-out tin cans and other odds and ends of junk. A rabbit hutch, improvised from an old chicken crate, stood on pegs against the house; and several moulting hens scratched at the packed earth beneath the trees. Two Negro boys, perhaps thirteen and fifteen respectively, were shucking beans into a kettle while a third boy—ten or thereabouts—looked on. I said, hello, and they leaped to their feet. The older boy placed himself in front of the other two. "Mammy," he called over his shoulder, not taking his eyes off me, "some white man heah."

There was trouble in the way he said white man. There was trouble in the woman who squeezed through the door and silently confronted me, hands on hips. I could see what Bob meant when he'd said she was plenty mean-looking.

This was going to be tough, as tough as it could be made on me. But I was thinking not so much of the fact as the causes that must lie behind it. What had been done to them, said and done to them, to make them like this?

I was wondering why Clinton had made that remark to me.

He'd apologized. He'd said he hadn't meant it, and I wanted to believe he hadn't. But why, unless he'd had it in his mind for a long time, had it slipped out so easily? How, unless a guy thinks a thing, can he say it?

Well . . . no matter. It wasn't deliberate, only an unfortunate slip of the tongue that was best forgotten. And I had forgotten it. At any rate, I certainly didn't hold any grudge.

president abraham lincoln jones 12

Funny lil man say, Howdy do, mam. My name Kozmi. I a turney. Mammy says, Huh. What at mean to me. Don need no a turney roun heah.

Lil man take pitcha out he pockit. You see iss boy befo, he say.

Mammy lookit pitcha. Mebbe, she say. Mebbe, no. He in trouble, huh.

Lil man say, Smattuh uh fack, he is, mam. You n yo childrin kin be uh great deal hep to me.

Mammy say, Huh. Why we hep white boy. Suhv he right.

Man kina frown. He say, But, mam. He say, mam, ats yo gahden up deah on hill.

Mammy say, Who say so. Mebbe ouah gahden, mebbe no. Mebbe we don know nuffin bout no gahden.

Man say, I got reason bleeve you up at gahden fo day ago. You n some uh yo childrin. You deah roun noon when iss boy pass by.

Mammy say, Who say we wuz.

Iss boy say you wuz, man say. Say sum uh you holiah at he.

Mammy say, Well, he say so, why you talkin uh me. Don remembah nuffin about it mahsef.

But you mus remembah, lil man say. Fo day ago roun noon. Vey impohtant you remembah, mam.

Mammy say, Who say I got to. Who it impohtant to, anyhow.

Man say, Possibly some yo childrin remembah, dese fine young men you have heah.

Mammy say, Dose deah fine young men don remembah nuffin I don.

Mistah John Brown kina push aroun Mammy. Mistah John Brown jus lil boy n he like at fine young men talk. He say, Mistah, I— n at all he say, cuz Mammy smack him spang in he mouf. She sock he so hahd he sail back, almos knock me n Genril Ulysses S. Grant ovah.

Lil man kina squirm, shuffle he feet. Lady, he say, I insis on ansuh. Eitha you tell me willingly uh I be foahced to take you inna cote.

Mammy say, Cote make uh puhsson remembah, huh. Since wen dey do at.

Lil man say, Yes, lady, dey insis you remembah. You do yo bes tuh remembah. All you jus say you don remembah, knowinly conceal evdunce fum cote you be in vey seious trouble.

Mammy say, Ats fine. Thanks fuh tellin me. Reckon we tells cote we nevah seen dat boy.

Lil man lookit me n Mistah n Genril. He look back at Mammy. Mammy kina grin at he. Well, she say, how you like us do dat.

Mam, lil man say, all I ast is simple ansuh to mah question. Suahly, at isn much to ast, jus simple yes oah no. Did you see iss boy roun noon fo days ago?

Tol you, Mammy say. Mebbe we see him, mebbe we didn.

Man muttuh somepn undah he bref. He kina look aroun. He say, Mam, you reelize dis lan city propehty. Some un make complain you not be heah vey long.

Some un make complain, Mammy say, some un gets in trouble day selves. I say dat some un thretn me, try make me say somepn ain so.

Well, lil man say.

Well, Mammy say. You got somepn else on yo min.

Lil man kina cleah he thoat. Kina look off uh one side uh Mammy. Mam, he say, mus be vey hahd livin dese cuhcumstances. How you like nice lil house close in. Some place mebbe yo childrin cn go tuh school n you cn fin wuk.

How I like, Mammy say. How I get, mistah.

Lil man say, Well, mam, I couln pay you tuh say you see iss boy. You unnerstan at, mam.

Mammy say, I unnerstans, mistah. I unnerstans, awright.

Lil man squirm. He say, I like be vey cleah on dis point. I could not n would not be pahty tuh procurin false witness. I wan nuffin fum you but de troof. Dey is no connection between whut you say n any sistance I give you.

Mammy grin. Sho dey ain, she say. We jus do it fo favuh.

Please, mam, man say. Dis not mattuh tuh joke about. It mus be unnerstood at—

Sho, Mammy laugh out loud. Who jokin, mistah.

Lil man lookt Mammy. Mammy laugh some mo. Lil man lookin like mebbe he go way but he don.

Well, Mammy say, whut you wan do, mistah.

Well, lil man say. I just wan be suah you unnerstood, mam.

Ain I said so, Mammy say. Mebbe we bettah go inside, mistah. You lookin kina peakid.

Lil man n Mammy go inside de house. Mistah John Brown staht cryin. Mistah John Brown jus lil ol boy, think mebbe man goin to huht Mammy. He say, He goin take Mammy way, Presdint. He goin lock huh up n shoot huh, Genril.

Hush yo mouf, I say. Cose he ain. What you think Mammy be doin while he doin at.

Bet he do. Mistah John Brown go on cryin. Lock huh up n shoot huh like dey done Pappy.

Genril Ulysses S. Grant give Mistah John Brown mean-eye. Tells him, Hush yo mouf, boy. Don do no talkin about Pappy. All us does is thinkin.

Lil man n Mammy comes out uh house. Mistah John Brown run n thow he ahms roun Mammy n Mammy stoop down n hol him. Lookit up at lil man.

Aw right, mistah, she say. We see you fust thing in mohnin. You wan somepn else.

Mam, lil man say. I do whut I say, regahdless, so will you

tell me, strickly fo my own infuhmation. Did you oah did you not see at boy.

Mammy don say nuffin. She jus stay stoopin down, huh ahms aroun Mistah John Brown. Just lookit lil man n grin, n she don say nuffin.

Lil man go way.

hargreave clinton 13

This was part of my mail (a very small part of it) on the Talbert-Eddleman case. The first item is a postal card, the others are letters:

Mr. D. A., dere sir, big red kilt that little edelmun girl. we sene her squatin down in the bushes there in the canyun an she had her close pult partways down an big red said o o thats fer me an he hopped off this frate. he is a mean sunabitch, sir, an done me plenty of dirt an i hop he gets the chare. canot tell you his rele name he got so minny but will probly be heddin fer west coast. L.A. or Seatle or mabe Frisco. big redhed fella an i sure hope you git him as he done plenty dirt to me. Awt to ben ded long ago . . .

Dear Sir:

This is purely hearsay, but from what I am told by a good friend of mine, I have strong doubts that Robert Talbert killed Josephine Eddleman. Rather, I incline to the belief that she may have met her well-deserved fate at the hands of some public-spirited citizen whom she seduced, such as this good friend of mine.

Now, sir, I cannot give you this man's name, but I assure you that he is a respectable business man and has a fine family of his own, and is absolutely trustworthy in every respect. He tells me that he was kind enough to offer Josephine a ride into the city one day, and she made such advances to him as he could not resist and intimacy resulted. Very foolishly and with the best of intentions, he was kind enough to give her his name and telephone afterwards. From then on he knew no peace. She would make appointments with this man, and deliberately fail to keep them. Or when she did keep them, she would tantalize this man until he was almost crazy and then withhold herself. Sometimes she would allow an intimacy, but not out of kindness or any sense of justice: only to keep him coming back so that she might torment him the more. As much as I hate to speak ill of the dead, she was an evil, wicked, spiteful little slut.

Now, sir, I cannot give you my name, and of course this is mere hearsay, more or less. But I am convinced that the Talbert boy is entirely innocent of this entirely justifiable homicide. I believe that this friend of mine, who is a very respected citizen and a fine family man, met Josephine by previous arrangement (possibly she had forgotten the appointment) and that driven to distraction by her sluttish wilfulness, he . . .

Dear Mr. Clinton:

I cannot tell you how I know without involving a third party, but Talbert is guilty. This is God's truth and I can make him admit it with full and irrefutable details. The story I will make him tell is nothing like the one he told you. My services will not cost you one red penny, and I GUARANTEE RESULTS. If interested, as I trust you will be, please address me as follows:

> "Mr. Switch,"
> c/o The Corporal Punishment Association,
> P.O.B. #798,
> City.

P.S. Can come any time, day or night.

Honored Sir:

Having recently received news in these parts that a

nigger, one Pearlie May Jones, and family of three nigger boys have given sworn depositions in the Eddleman murder case, I feel duty bound to advise you that this wench is beyond doubt the most uppity, no-account nigger in the country and the truth is not in her nor in anyone related to her. The whole family are liars, malingerers and scalawags. I would not believe one of them on a stack of Bibles.

This outfit, which formerly included the husband and father, one Union Victory Jones, were at one time croppers on my plantation. They were always biggity and back-talky, and I would not ordinarily have had them around for five minutes, but the war was on and niggers were hard to come by. I was finally compelled to take steps when the man accused my storekeeper of giving him false weight.

I ordered him to leave the plantation forthwith. He surlily refused to do so until his crop was in, and he used very bad language to the sheriff whom I summoned to evict him. He was promptly arrested and taken to jail, where, I am not sorry to say, he was killed in an escape attempt. He was a plain bad nigger. His family is just as uppity and no-account as he was. They hate whites, but they have an even greater hatred of the law. Given the chance to obstruct justice, as they were in this case, I have not the slightest doubt that . . .

. . . It was after midnight. I was sitting in the kitchen with a cup of hot milk when Arlene came down the backstairs and peered in at me. Arlene is the peering, peeking type. She is incapable of the direct approach, sans tiptoeing, twittering and head-tilting. I seem to remember a time when I thought her mannerisms charming; on a woman of fifty, with her hair in curlers and several ounces of cream on her face, the less said about them the better.

"Dear," she said, coming in, "shouldn't you be in bed?"

"I'm all right," I said. "I'll be up after a while."

"But you must get your sleep, darling. You know you won't feel right tomorrow if you don't."

I didn't say anything. She has made that remark to me at least ten thousand times, and I can never think of a reply. I wonder why it is that supposedly intelligent men, men of at least better-than-average intelligence, will always marry the stupidest women they can find.

She sat down at the table next to me, "cuddled" is the word she would use, squeezing so close that I could smell the face cream and the vinegary odor of the hair-curling lotion. For a moment I was afraid she might attempt to "steal a sip" of my milk, but fortunately she forbore. I seem to have her pretty well broken of that particular kind of cuteness.

"Some more of those awful letters, darling?" She wrinkled her nose in distaste. "Why do you keep reading them, anyway? There's never anything in them but viciousness and ugly things."

"I believe I've explained," I said, "that it's my duty to read them. Some one of these people who write in may have proof of Talbert's guilt or innocence."

"But you already know he's innocent! You know you do, dear."

I sighed and shook my head. "Do I?" I said. "Well, thank you, Arlene. You've taken a very great load off my mind."

"But, dear. You said—"

"All right," I said. "I believe I did feel in the beginning that there was not a very strong case against the boy, but the situation has changed since then. Can you grasp that thought, Arlene? It isn't actually too complex. Can you understand that circumstances change, that what is true one day may not be true the next?"

"We-l"—obviously she couldn't understand it; it was too deep for her—"-but what about that Negro family, darling? You said—"

"Please. *Please*, Arlene!" I said. "Must you keep quoting me? Can't I ever make an offhand remark without your throwing it up to me later? What are you supposed to be, my wife or my conscience?"

"Now, darling . . ." She laughed trillingly. "You know you did say that—"

"I said it *then*," I sighed. "*Then*, Arlene, at the time Kossmeyer discovered the family and got their story. I thought it was reasonably conclusive, and I believed the public would think it was. Since the public apparently wasn't and isn't completely convinced, I may have been wrong. At any rate, I can't dismiss the case."

She nodded slowly. Her forehead puckered in a frown, creasing the face cream into white, greasy little worms.

"I see," she said. "Then, it doesn't really matter whether he's guilty or not, does it? Whether he could actually prove that he was innocent? It isn't what he is, but what other people are. If they say he's guilty—"

"They don't say so," I said. "They simply don't say that he's innocent. They're not convinced that he is. I"—I hesitated—"I don't understand it myself, all this furor in the newspapers. They've wrung the thing for all it's worth and then some, but yet they keep on. One following the other, one trying to outdo the other. I know how it got started, but—"

"But, dear. You said you weren't influenced by the newspapers. You've always said that."

"All right," I said.

"But you did, dear! I don't know how many times I've heard you say that—"

"Oh, come now," I said. "Surely, you've kept count. Go on and tell me, Arlene: how many times have I said that I wasn't influenced by the newspapers?"

"Silly!" She forced a laugh. "Now you're teasing me, aren't you?"

I turned and looked at her. I gave her a long, slow look, letting my eyes move over her face, letting her see them move a little at a time. Letting her see what I saw.

Then, I looked away and picked up my milk.

She was silent for what must have been more than a minute. She hardly seemed to be breathing. And yet her laughter went on. I could feel her shoulder shiver against mine, sense, without seeing, the rigor mortis-like contortions of body and face. She rocked back and forth, proving herself blithe and unhurt, unaware of intended hurt, silencing the sounds that would have denied the actions.

It was a splendid piece of acting; I doubt that Bernhardt could have done it as well. But, then, I doubt that the Divine Sarah ever repeated a scene so often as Arlene has this one. I don't mean to imply that it is the only bit in her repertoire. She has others, The Helpless Child, The Winsome Weeper, The Dignified Doormat, et cetera, and all very effective, too—for, perhaps, the first few hundred times you see them. But she surpasses herself as the Mute and Mirthful Martyr. Practice has made her well nigh perfect.

"W-Well . . ." She spoke at last, getting a gasping tremoloish note into her voice. "Y-You see what you do to me, dear? You simply mustn't tease me any more."

"If you're at all interested," I said. "I'd like to set the record straight on my attitude toward the newspapers."

"Of course, darling. I'd love to have you. Not that you need to do it on my account, but—"

"I'm not influenced by the newspapers, but I am by public opinion as reflected in the newspapers. They don't mold it or make that opinion, to any great extent, but they do reflect it. They're a barometer of what the public wants, or is about to want. They may get a little ahead of the public, but they're never behind it. They're never greatly in disagreement with it. When they are, they get in agreement quickly or they go out of business. . . . Do you understand what I'm saying, Arlene?"

"Of course. Certainly, dear." She nodded earnestly. "Not influenced by newspapers . . . only what's in newspapers. Is that right, darling?"

"You know it isn't!" I said. "You're deliberately twisting my words. What I said was that—that—oh, to hell with it."

"Poor darling." She patted my arm. "I just hate myself for being so silly and stupid when you have so many troubles."

"Well, forget it," I said. "Maybe that Federal judgeship will come through soon enough to take me off the hook. If, that is, it comes through at all. Kossmeyer is doing everything he can, but . . ."

But I wouldn't blame him if he didn't. I wouldn't blame him if he actually blocked the appointment, made me look like such an abysmal idiot that I'd be dropped from consideration. He could do it. I'd look like seven kinds of a malicious, bigoted fool if I was forced to rip into that Negro woman and her three children, make her look like a liar, a malcontent, an ignorant spiteful—

All Kossmeyer had to do was sit back and let me cut my own throat.

"Darling . . ."

"Yes?" I said.

"What will happen to the boy if—when—you get the appointment? If the case is still pending, I mean?"

"I don't know," I said. "My successor will have to take care of it."

"Oh," she said. "Yes, I suppose it would be his responsibility."

I turned and looked at her. I said, "If you want something to worry about, Arlene, I'll gladly help you out. Would you like me to do that, give you some suggestions for personal improvement before you start improving others?"

"Oh, you!" she laughed. "Now, you just stop teasing me, dear."

"Go to bed," I said. "Do you hear me, Arlene? I want you to go to bed. *Now!*"

And, of course, she chose deliberately to misunderstand me.

"Mmm," she said, getting up lingeringly. "Oh, you naughty bad boy, you!"

She moved around the table and struck a pose in front of me—Seduction in Sheer Silk (or, more accurately, Circe in Curlers and Cream). And I had to look away quickly, or burst into laughter, and there are some things you cannot laugh about.

She'd never put on any weight. She still had that "cute figure" . . . as they'd spoken of it in the 'twenties. Flat-chested, hipless, thighs hinged to her torso. A build like a clothespin.

You could have laid a thick book, even a Blackstone, flat in her crotch without crimping the binding.

I kept my eyes on the table, forced them to stay there. After a time, I heard the kitchen door open, but there was no sound of its closing.

"Arlene," I said. "I asked you to go to bed. Please."

"Isn't it terrible?" she said, slowly. "Isn't it terrible? You're just like you always were, the very same person, and suddenly that isn't good enough any more. Now, it's bad. You're no good, you're treated like you're no good, and there's nothing you can do to defend yourself. Nothing you can say or do. You were good—you thought you were and you tried to be—and you never stop trying—but now you're bad. And you're punished for it . . . forever and forever."

I looked up at last. I managed a fairly pleasant smile.

"Don't worry any more about it," I said. "The newspapers can't keep up their racket much longer. Talbert's going to be all right."

"Talbert?" she said blankly. "Tal—Oh, of course! I'm so sorry, darling. I guess I was thinking of someone else. . . ."

Herself.

donald skysmith 14

It was about five in the morning when I reached the office. The charwomen had just finished their cleaning, leaving the Venetian blinds drawn high and all the lights burning.

I got the bottle out of my desk and drew a chair up to the windows. I sat there, drinking and smoking, staring out over the city, watching the red spears of sunlight stab through the horizon and splinter into shimmering motes of silvery yellow. Dawn, the slow unsheathing of a sword; then, the untempered effulgence of day, rapacious, brutal, striking away the merciful shadows, challenging the pygmy man to battle, daring him to look yet again upon his handiwork and pronounce it good.

I sat there for a long time—until it was not I who looked out at the city but the city that looked in at me. I moved back. I got up and wandered aimlessly around the room, and still it looked in at me. Appraising me, thoughtfully, studying the Rhodes scholar, the Guggenheim fellow, the Pulitzer prize-winner, the managing editor; those things— this thing—this peculiar and puzzling animal that was Donald Skysmith.

Able bodied? Yes, he was able-bodied. Intelligent? Well, yes. One would have to assume so. Kindly, a man of good heart? Of course. Certainly.

Well, why then? Why had *the* Donald Skysmith become this Donald Skysmith? What had happened to him? What had he been trying to get?

And what had he got?

I looked around the office. I lowered the blinds and drew their slats tight, and I turned off all the lights.

That was better. The burning in my eyes grew less painful, and there was some small surcease from the blinding brain-splitting headache.

I sat down at the desk, and pillowed my head on my arms.

I hadn't had any sleep last night. Teddy had taken a sudden turn for the worse shortly after I reached home, and it was not until one in the morning that—that the doctor had left. The children were very wakeful and in need of reassuring about Teddy. By the time I got them sufficiently soothed to be turned over to their nurse, sleep was impossible for myself. Probably it would have been impossible, anyway.

Teddy . . . Theodora . . . poor teddy-bear . . .

But she was all right, now. She'd be swell from now on. As good now—in a way—as she used to be, laughing and cutting up, carrying on as much over a sack of popcorn as you would a ten-course banquet. God, I could hear her, now, the shrieks and squeals, the oohs and ohs and ahs, the giggles and snickers, the wondrous and wondering delight in simply being alive. I could feel the thin arms hug-

ging around my neck, see the too-large eyes laughing inno-
cently into mine. I marveled that I could ever have got
annoyed with her, a little irritated and ever-so-slightly bored.
It was such a short time, really, since we'd been together.
Hardly more than yesterday, it seemed, since our marriage.

I was working in Oklahoma City—no, it was Tulsa. Hell,
how could I get mixed up on a thing like that? And, Teddy,
well, let's see . . . oh, yes . . . Teddy was going to the uni-
versity there and working as a part-time teller in a bank.
That's how I met her. I cashed my paycheck there, and it
just seemed a step from that to getting her in bed. And I
didn't know until it was too late that she was virginal.
Teddy thought it was a wonderful joke on me. She thought
it was wonderful period. She squealed and groaned so
ecstatically that my landlady came up and pounded on the
door . . . Well, I had a short payday that week. Some lousy
loan shark had garnisheed my wages. But Teddy had a
pretty good watch and a heavy gold crucifix, so we hocked
those and caught a bus into Kansas. We barely had enough
for the trip, the license and the j.p.'s fee. . . . She was preg-
nant the first month, and I think that must have marked the
beginning of the cancer, because, of course, anything but
an abortion was out of the question, and we didn't have the
money for a good one. She bled for days on end until I
didn't see how a drop of blood could be left in her. And
long after the bleeding stopped, the pain continued. Night
after night, I sat with her on my lap, holding her and rocking her as you might rock a baby. It was the only way she
could go to sleep, the only thing that helped the pain. It
was as though part of the pain went out of her and came
into me, and we shared it together. Some nights we were
like that all night long, and with every creak of the rocker
the one thought burned deeper and deeper into my mind. I
made a song out of it, a song that was a promise . . . *Never
again, Teddy, never again, my teddy-bear. No more pain for Don's
sweet Teddy, never, never ever, teddy-bear.* That was the way it
went, something along that order, and then there was the
refrain . . . *Bye, bye, bye-oh-beddy, sleep, sleep, my little Teddy.
Sleep, sleep, my sweet . . .*

. . . The phone was ringing. I snatched up the receiver and answered before my eyes were opened. Habit, you know: the fire-horse lunging into harness at the sound of the bell. There was no practical reason for politeness and promptness.

It was the Captain. He went on talking to the operator.

"You're very sure, now, miss? He's the genuine Donald Skysmith?"

"He, hee, hee! Y-Yes, sir. It's Mr. Skysmith, sir."

"You're positive, are you? There's no chance that he might be an impostor?"

"Yes, sir, I'm sure. Tee, hee, hee . . ."

I raised the receiver up to arm's length, took careful aim and crashed it down into the cradle as hard as I could. I hoped it burst their God damned eardrums. I hoped it knocked that bitch off her chair and that son-of-a-bitch out of his half-acre bed. The lousy, filthy, rotten, bastardly, Fascistic old fart. I'd get that whoremonger, yet! By God, I'd get him yet! I'd swing those God damned floozies by the heels, beat the piss out of him with his own floozies. And then I'd make a pile out of them with him at the top and burn the whole shideree to a cinder. I'd . . .

The phone was ringing again. I looked at it dully. . . . Beat him, burn him? Why, when he was already doing so much worse to himself? He must be, you know. He had to be. Sensibility presupposes sensitivity. One cannot be at once sensible and insensible. He did nothing without thinking it through carefully, without complete realization of the consequences. He had to know what he was doing. Knowingly, he created a hell of wretchedness and violence, bigotry, ignorance and class hatred, and the knowledge of what he had deliberately created must be more searing than the hell itself.

But why? Why was he the way he was? Well, why was I? And don't we all dig our hells?

I lifted the receiver and said, "Hello, Captain."

"Ah, Don," he said. "How are you this morning?"

"I'm all right," I said.

"And Teddy? What about Teddy, Don?"

"She's all right, now," I said. "She was never better, in fact. She gave me a little message to pass on to you just before she—went to sleep last night."

"That's very touching, Don. What was the message?"

I told him. And, no, I wasn't making it up. I used her exact words.

"Here it is, Captain. She said, 'Tell the old horse's ass to kiss mine.'"

"Wonderful!" he laughed softly. "A wonderful girl, Teddy. I liked her from the moment I met her, and I don't like many people."

"That's quite a coincidence, isn't it?" I said.

The phone seemed to go completely dead for a few moments. If anyone but the Captain had been on the wire, I'd have thought he'd hung up. But the Captain never did things that way. When the Captain was through with you, he said so. Until he did say so . . .

My heart began to pound with a kind of dull excitement, with hope and something akin to self-horror. I still wanted my job? I was still willing—anxious—to go on, if I was allowed to?

He cleared his throat, hesitated for a second to get my attention. "It's difficult, isn't it, Don? A graphic illustration of Darwin's soundness. Man may be uncomfortable in the trees, but he's by nature a climbing animal. He—you still must live, get ahead."

The excitement was growing, and the horror with it. I wanted to stay on here, work, live, get ahead, climb—and I hated myself for wanting to.

"I don't know, Don," he said, quietly. "I'd like to think about it a few minutes. Meanwhile—what happened on this Talbert story? I never intended for you to go to such extreme lengths. You knew I didn't. We were after our opposition, not the boy. Why did you make such a thoroughgoing botch of things?"

"I . . ." I stared down at the desk, trying to come to a decision. "It's jumped our circulation, Captain."

"As much as it's lost? Does the temporary jump in news-stand sales offset what we've lost, the alienation of a large block of solid, regular readers? I don't think so, Don. And you haven't answered my question."

"I don't think I need to," I said. "You already know just as you know everything else that happens here."

"Yes," he said, "I already know. But there's one thing I don't know, Don. I can't understand why you allowed a man like Willis to remain on the *Star*, a man who apparently was shrewder than you. That was very bad management. One of the first concerns of an efficient executive is to eliminate potential competition."

"Willis is a good newspaper man," I said. "I had no reason to fire him."

"Ah, Don. You disappoint me more and more."

"I tried to promote him," I said, "when he was organizing the union. He laughed at me."

"Perhaps you didn't offer him anything good enough, Don."

"Perhaps I didn't."

He sighed. I could picture the thoughtful, calculating look on his vulture's face. "Getting back to the Talbert story, Don. You were over a barrel, but why stay over it? Why haven't you swung the other way, gone over to the boy's side, started a defense fund for him—given him the treatment in reverse? That would give us another jump on the opposition. It would get back our solid circulation, and we're going to *have* to do it. We're going to free the boy. Why haven't you done it before this?"

A story, that's all the boy was. The story had run out, and we needed another. "Only one reason," I said. "I wasn't smart enough."

"I see . . ." he murmured. "Well, the realization itself contains a great deal of wisdom. Perhaps . . ."

"Yes, sir," I said. *And was there eagerness in my voice?* "Yes, Captain?"

"I don't know, Don. Perhaps you've never needed to be prodded, to have a club swung at you. It was at my hand so I used it, but possibly it wasn't necessary. You might even do much better without it. I think . . . I think I'd like to have you step over to the windows, Don. Stick your head out."

"Sir?" I said.

"You heard me. Put your head out the window. Then come back and tell me whether it is raining."

"No!" I said. "No I—it's not necessary, sir. I know it isn't raining."

"Don."

"No! I tell you it isn't—"

I heard it, then. The gust of wind, the drops striking against the panes.

I waited. And again there was that long dead silence. And then, at last, another sigh. "You're guilty of a very common failing, Don. Fear of symbols. You think I make a puppet out of you. You don't like it. You're humiliated. Degradation by association. And yet, all I'm doing is testing you, your powers of observation. To get ahead, to climb, you've got to observe. Still . . . You must be very tired. You must be very, very tired. I suggest you go downstairs and get yourself a cup of coffee."

"N-No! No," I said. "Who the hell do you think you are, anyway? Who the hell do you think you are? Do you think you're God?"

"Yes. Don't you think that you are? Get the coffee, Don."

"Y-Yes, sir," I said. "Yes, Captain."

I laid the receiver on the desk. Very gently. I went out through the city room, and down on the elevator to the lobby. I walked blindly down the street toward the lunchroom.

I came to it, and I passed it by. And I entered a bar.

I sat down on one of the leather-covered stools, and ordered a double Scotch with water.

I was down near the bottom of the drink when a waiter touched my shoulder.

I followed him to the telephone.

"Yes, Captain?" I said.

"The club was necessary, wasn't it, Don?" he said. "You have to be driven, and now I have nothing to drive you with. No way of bringing pressure on you. I can't use Teddy's health any more. Nothing to tempt you or make you afraid or make you work harder."

"Nothing," I said, "and it feels good."

"Your desk is being cleared out, Don, and the business office is preparing your check. If you'll just remain where you are, a copy boy will be down with everything within the next few minutes."

"It's nine-thirty," I said. "I expect to be paid for every damned minute I have to wait."

"I assumed you would. You'll find the check takes care of your salary through nine-forty-five. And, Don . . ."

"Well?" I said.

He was silent.

"Spit it out!" I said. "What have you got to say?"

He coughed apologetically. He didn't sound at all like the Captain.

"I'm afraid I can't say it, Don. I don't seem to be able to find the words to express what I feel. All I can say is that I'm sorry. I was very sorry to learn of Teddy's death."